WISH UPON A DUKE

ERICA RIDLEY

Erica Ridley

ISBN: 1943794545
ISBN-13: 978-1943794546
Copyright © 2018 Erica Ridley
Photograph on cover © PeriodImages

Welcome to Christmas!

Our picturesque village is nestled around Marlowe Castle, high atop the gorgeous mountain we call home. Cressmouth is best known for our year-round Yuletide cheer. Here, we're family.

The legend of our twelve dukes? Absolutely true! But perhaps not always in the way one might expect…

CHAPTER 1

Marlowe Castle
Christmas, England

"This way, please." Miss Gloria Godwin ushered this month's crop of stargazers away from the light spilling from the castle's front doors.

This evening, only a dozen individuals braved the crisp winter weather in search of stars. The few Gloria did not recognize were tourists. Each time she took a new group, she hoped the future love of her life would be among them.

Cupid hadn't struck yet, but surely it was just a matter of time.

The town of Cressmouth was better known as Christmas. Their perpetually snow-dusted mountaintop village was a favorite holiday spot for those willing to trek up to the northernmost corner of England to enjoy its charms.

The majority of faces in tonight's crowd belonged to children of local parents taking advantage of a free hour whilst their offspring were entertained elsewhere. Some of the children had attended these outings since they started. By now, they were old friends.

"For those of you joining us for the first time," she began with a smile, "welcome to the sky-walk. Tonight, we will exercise our brains as well as our legs, as we—"

"May I tell?" A young girl with a woolen cap and thick scarf bounced on her toes.

Gloria gave an encouraging nod. "Go ahead, Annie."

"On the first walk, we learn the names of the stars and the stories behind their constellations." Annie's eyes sparkled. "And on the second walk—"

"We get to make up our own!" six-year-old Nigel blurted out in glee. "We can even wish upon a star!"

"That's right," Gloria said with a laugh. "If this is your first time star-gazing, memorizing hundreds of names and configurations can seem overwhelming. But never fear! Raise your hand if you've ever lain on grass in order to pick out shapes in the clouds."

Everyone lifted a fur muff or a woolen mitten.

"Star-gazing is similar." Gloria smiled at her group. "Should you forget the North Star is Polaris inside Ursa Minor, you may remember a simpler story and still be able to find the right direction when you need it."

Two of the tourists exchanged a loving look. Their obvious romantic connection warmed Gloria's heart.

"Miss Godwin's father was a Captain for the Royal Navy," Annie gushed. "He taught her everything."

Gloria swallowed a lump in her throat at the reminder. "And Annie was my very first sky-walker. She'll be happy to answer questions, too. Shall we wait another moment in case there are latecomers?"

She glanced over her shoulder at the castle entrance and forgot whatever else she'd been about to say.

The dashing Mr. Christopher Pringle was standing at the open doors, bathed in light from the crystal chandeliers just inside. She had almost had a chance to meet him two weeks ago, during a party at the castle to celebrate her friend's latest perfume.

Instead, she'd remained a wallflower. There had been no one to properly introduce them. All she could do was admire him from afar.

And, *oh*, was there plenty to admire.

Dark brown hair. Snowy white neckcloth. Black superfine coat cut to accentuate broad shoulders. Gorgeous buckskins that clung to the muscles of his legs. Gleaming Hessians. Adonis, come to life.

Her pulse skipped. Was he coming on her tour? Would she finally get to meet him?

Until a fortnight ago, all she knew about Christopher Pringle was hearsay and a too-brief listing in Debrett's Peerage. His elder brother was London's most infamous rake and heir presumptive to a dukedom, making the younger Mr. Pringle second in line to their cousin's title.

Like his rakish brother, he spent his Seasons in London and was every bit as mind-meltingly handsome in the flesh. There the similarities ended.

While his brother's infamy was due to countless seductions in Society boudoirs, Christopher Pringle was far more mysterious. His name never graced scandal columns, and his antics— whatever they might be—had not once been immortalized in a penny caricature.

Gloria's heart stopped. *He was looking right at her.*

She forced her suddenly frozen features into a welcoming smile.

He didn't smile back.

She added an encouraging wave of her fingers. A friendly little *come-on-over, the-stars-are-fine*. And an even wider smile.

His expression did not change.

He didn't see her, she realized in mortification. He was staring right at her, but his mind was on something more interesting, his thoughts a thousand miles away.

"Miss Godwin?" one of the tourists asked hesitantly.

Gloria's cheeks flushed with heat. Heaven help her. The group had caught her gawking at one of the castle guests as though he were a celestial being she'd just discovered.

"Let's go," she said quickly, hurrying them out of sight from the castle doors before she could make a bigger cake of herself. "Overhead, do you see the three bright stars in a crooked line?"

The only reason Gloria was able to give a flawless introduction to the stars visible in tonight's sky was because she knew each one as if it were family. Their habits, their secrets, in which positions and seasons they were most likely to appear. None escaped her notice.

Her smile faltered. Perhaps she felt such a kinship with the stars because she, too, was always present and just as forgettable.

As they did with the constellations above, gentlemen might repeat her name, possibly even note her general appearance, and then immediately confuse her with any other nondescript young lady they'd ever met. Time after time, they looked right at her without ever registering what they were seeing.

Exactly like Christopher Pringle.

Her chest tightened. Just once, Gloria wished a gentleman would become entranced with her at first sight. Or speak to her. Or recall her enough to pick her out from a crowd. It would be the first step toward finding love.

"The constellation to the right," she continued, "is known as Leo. Who can tell me what's special about this formation?"

That was what she wanted. To be special. To be remembered. To be actively sought out.

And yes, a part of her hoped whoever finally noticed her would be as dashing as Mr. Pringle.

"Imbecile," she muttered.

The tourists snapped startled gazes in her direction.

"I said 'sea serpent,'" she corrected smoothly, pointing overhead. "Some know the constellation Hydra by that name. If you trace the undulating pattern…"

Clearly, Christopher Pringle was in no danger of falling in love with her at first sight. She was not as distraught as might be expected, given how much she yearned for her happy ever after.

Mr. Pringle was an unknown factor. Handsome but risky.

Despite him arriving in town two weeks earlier, one of the reasons Gloria hadn't contrived to throw herself directly in his path was the possibility that he was as transient as his rakish brother.

But now that England's most unrepentant rake appeared to be falling tail-over-teakettle in love with her dear friend Penelope, Gloria couldn't help but reconsider. Better yet, she would soon have someone who could introduce her to gentlemen like Mr. Pringle.

If it happened under exactly the right circumstances… well, a dreamer like Gloria wasn't ready to rule out love-at-second-sight quite yet.

"And lastly," she said as they neared the end of the first trek about the castle, "who can tell me the name of this handsome beast in the northern sky?"

"Duke!" Nigel blurted in triumph.

"We're not doing wishes yet," Annie scolded him, then puffed out her chest. "Draco, the dragon."

"Just so." Gloria lifted her palm toward the stars. "The curve to the right represents—"

"Why did he say 'Duke?'" asked one of the tourists.

"He's ahead of the game." Gloria pinched Nigel's grinning cheek. "When I was little, I misheard several constellation names, and believed for years that 'Draco' was actually 'Duke'. My father found my mispronunciations amusing and adopted the new names as a private joke."

"He taught you to always wish upon a star," Annie said.

"That's right. And I always choose Duke. The creature right up there."

Every single night. Gloria smiled up at the stars. One day, it would be her turn.

"Is it time to make a wish?" Nigel begged. "Please?"

"Very well," she answered with a laugh. "We'll take our second tour in the opposite direction, so that we may start with Draco. Do you see a dragon?"

"I see a duke," he answered immediately. "Just like you. And I wish for a hobbyhorse."

Annie rolled her eyes. "You always wish for toys. I wish for a rapier, so I might learn to fence."

"That's not practical at all," laughed one of the other girls. "I wish for an embroidery set."

"What a charming custom!" A lady tourist lay her head on her husband's shoulder as they stared up at the sky together. "No wonder people fall in love with this quaint village."

Nigel turned to face her. "But what do you wish for?"

"Why, to stay here forever," the lady answered immediately. She gazed at her husband. "Darling, we must purchase a local cottage so that we have a permanent home here in Christmas."

Gloria gave a practiced smile as the other tourists gushed their agreement. Everyone always "fell in love" and wished to stay "forever."

But none of them ever did.

"What about you, Miss Godwin?" Annie asked. "What do you wish for?"

"To visit the stars," Gloria answered automatically.

The children groaned. "That's what you always wish for!"

Gloria tousled their woolen caps and led the group forward. They were wrong. Visiting the stars was never what Gloria wanted. It was only what she dared say aloud.

Tonight, just like every night, the same wish had erupted from her chest and burst toward the stars.

To be noticed.

CHAPTER 2

*M*r. Christopher Pringle reluctantly returned his attention to Marlowe Castle's bustling reception hall. There was time. The sky would be cloudless and brilliant many other nights. In just a few weeks, he'd have more than enough opportunity to gaze up at the stars on his long trip across the sea. First things first.

He had a fortnight left in Christmas, and he intended to make the most of it.

"There you are, Pringle!" One of his new friends clapped him on the shoulder. "What say you to a game of billiards over at Skeffington's?"

The other gentlemen voiced their agreement. "Rumor has it, Skeffington's wine collection could rival the castle's cellar. Shall we go make quick work of it?"

To their obvious dismay, Christopher motioned them ahead. "You'll have to start without me, I'm afraid. I may drop by later."

"Who knows if there will still be any wine

left?" they teased him as they jostled each other out the castle exit and into the night.

As fond as he'd become of the local gentlemen, Christopher was glad to see them go. He was here in search of a bride, not a lads' night out. The fewer excess eligible bachelors crowding the reception hall, the better.

He surveyed his surroundings. The hunt was not going well. Although he had been in Christmas for two weeks, all of the female attention had been focused on his elder brother, an inveterate rake. Even this far north, "Saint Nick's" wickedness was as legendary as his conquests. The mere sight of his chiseled visage was enough to make a young lady swoon.

Or to make Christopher bury his face in his palms. He was ready to finally have his turn.

"Mr. Pringle?" came a soft feminine voice from behind him.

He turned around with a wide smile. "Why, Miss Borland, you look fetching tonight. Is that a new bonnet?"

Her cheeks flushed pink. "I thought… Is Nicholas here?"

Christopher's smile tightened. It was not the first time he'd been confused for his popular brother. He ought to accustom himself to being second best.

"I'm afraid he's elsewhere this evening." Christopher couldn't be more specific. He loved his brother and had been sworn to secrecy.

"Oh." The young lady's disappointment was palpable.

She all but ran away before Christopher could offer to escort her to the refreshment buffet on the other side of the receiving hall.

He tried not to take the implicit rejection personally. Living in the shadow of a devilishly handsome rake who also happened to be heir presumptive to a dukedom meant that no matter what Christopher did, he was relegated to the background. Whenever Nick was around, Christopher became invisible.

So, he'd stopped sticking around. "Saint Nick Fever" taking over England? Christopher visited Sicily, Barcelona, Vienna. His heart sang just thinking about the incredible experiences he'd had exploring other lands.

Travel was in his soul. But he hadn't lost the dream of wanting to share the adventure with a wife.

Speaking of which, a lovely young lady was headed right in his direction.

He made an elegant leg. "How are you this evening, Miss Quincy?"

"Splendid, thank you." She glanced over his shoulder. "Are you here with your brother?"

He kept his smile in place. "I fear Nicholas has other plans this evening."

Miss Quincy's face fell, but at least she managed to curtsey before hurrying elsewhere.

Christopher tried not to feel discouraged.

This trip was meant to be the perfect opportunity to bride-hunt. A cozy, secluded mountaintop village in the northernmost point of the country; a world away from the London social whirl his brother dominated.

Yet the moment Christopher had set out on the journey, Nick had decided to join in. They were brothers. They didn't spend enough time together. A joint holiday would surely be the ticket.

It was not.

Not only had Nick become the instant obsession of every unwed female within town limits, he'd even managed to be the first to fall in love. The banns would begin on the morrow at the local parish church. It was nothing short of a miracle.

Christopher was thrilled for his brother, and more than a little relieved for himself. Once word got loose that Nick was off the market, everything would change. Christopher rolled back his shoulders in relief.

Tomorrow morning, he would finally know what it was like to live a normal life.

"The wind blows not from the east or the west, but from deep within," came a dreamy voice to his right.

Virginia Underwood.

He could have hugged her in relief. He and Virginia were merely friends, but at least she hadn't approached in search of his brother.

Christopher gave his deepest bow. "How are you this evening?"

"My cat is restless." Her head tilted. "Perhaps I should take him to the aviary."

"Perhaps not," Christopher suggested hurriedly. "The population is low enough as it stands."

She thought this over, then nodded. "I'll wait until there's another bird."

"Miss Underwood, who is your friend?" a merry voice boomed behind them.

They turned to grin at Fred Fawkes, a white-haired gentleman who had clerked in the castle's counting house for decades until old age impaired his ability to continue. Although Christopher had been introduced on at least three other occasions, Mr. Fawkes never failed to be welcoming and jolly.

"You remember Chris Pringle," Virginia shouted into the old man's ear.

Mr. Fawkes frowned. "Kris Kringle, you say?"

She took his ear trumpet and placed it to his head. "*Mr. Pringle.*"

"Mr. Pringle!" The old clerk beamed at Christopher. "Do you like Christmas?"

"Very much," Christopher answered immediately. He wasn't certain whether Mr. Fawkes referred to the holiday or the town, but in either case the answer was an enthusiastic yes.

What was there not to like about a winter wonderland where one could experience the joys of Christmastide year-round? Not that he would stay that long, of course. Coming to this castle was like visiting another country. Marvelous for the first month, and then his feet itched to be off on the next adventure.

"May I fetch either of you a refreshment

from the buffet?" he asked, ensuring he kept his words loud and crisp for Mr. Fawkes.

The old clerk chortled with more mirth than the comment deserved. "I'll take care of that myself."

"What did he think I said?" Christopher whispered to Virginia as the elderly gentleman ambled toward the spiral stair leading to the guest wings.

Virginia gazed back with wide eyes. "Can we ever truly know another's mind?"

"Fair enough." He felt his spirits rise. "Perhaps the night is improving. You and Mr. Fawkes were the first to approach without inquiring after my brother's whereabouts."

"I know where he is." Her smile was self-satisfied. "The turtledove has found its nest."

Christopher had never thought of his brother as particularly birdlike, but the analogy was otherwise sound. After a lifetime of flitting from bed to bed, Nick had finally found his permanent home.

"Now it is up to you to find yours," Virginia added.

"I am on the hunt," Christopher assured her.

She cast a skeptical glance about the castle's luxurious reception hall. More footmen than guests remained. The vaulted ceiling and vast interior only made the emptiness more profound.

At this time of the evening, most of the villagers were either abed, or wherever they intended to pass the night. The castle's kitchen would keep the refreshment buffet stocked at all hours, but the party was clearly over.

"I may not meet my bride tonight," he acknowledged.

Virginia graciously refrained from saying, *Obviously.*

"I must bid you goodnight," she murmured instead. "I must take my cat for a walk."

"Not to the aviary," he reminded her.

She nodded. "Perhaps next week."

After Virginia headed upstairs, Christopher turned toward the exit. Although he, too, was staying in the castle—it was the only "inn" for miles—he was far from ready to retire. Night was when the heavens came alive.

His jaw tightened. If his prized telescope hadn't been damaged on the trip north, he'd stay out until dawn admiring the sky.

Especially on a night as clear as this one.

With determination, he strode to the castle exit to see how many stars he could spy with his bare eyes. A movement not far ahead caught his interest.

Just across the garden stood a cluster of about a dozen individuals, all with their heads tilted skyward and their fingers pointing above them.

He stepped closer in surprise. This far from London, he was usually the only gentleman astronomer about. This motley group appeared comprised of adults and children, male and female alike.

He turned to one of the door attendants.

"Have you any idea what those people are doing?"

"Sky-walk," the footman replied without hesitation. "First Saturday of every month, castle guests tour the grounds, peering up at the stars."

A sky-walk.

Christopher's pulse skipped in pleasure. He could not think of anything more noble than instilling young people with respect for and knowledge of the stars. It was a calling he took quite seriously.

Indeed, if travel was his passion, astronomy was his obsession. When a few like-minded scholars had written to inform him that they hoped to found a society of gentlemen astronomers, it had almost been enough to tempt him back to London for an extra month or two.

Adventuring might introduce a man to foreign tongues, cuisine, and cultures, but the one constant in any far-flung corner of the globe was the sky overhead. Each constellation, each celestial body, was more familiar to him than his own reflection.

His pulse hummed. That he should discover twin souls in a sparsely populated Christmas village, of all places... He hurried forward without waiting to summon his greatcoat. He could not let an opportunity to befriend fellow aficionados pass him by.

As he neared the circle, it became quickly apparent that the leader of the sky-walk was not a fellow gentleman astronomer, as Christopher had presumed, but a beautiful young woman. A *lady* astronomer. His heart thumped. He had never met a female scholar of the stars.

This one had thick black curls, a truly sensuous mouth, and a sensible fur-lined pelisse to protect her from the weather. Christopher was still too far away to discern the words of her current lecture. He gave up all pretense of nonchalance and began to lope across the garden to catch up with the group and meet their delightful leader in person.

The conservative science-minded men of his acquaintance had long pooh-poohed the idea of a woman learning the intricacies of the stars, but obviously they had never met—

"That's right, Annie," the lady astronomer was saying to a child. "We *do* call the brightest star in the sky 'Brummell' because it's as shiny as a dandy's spangled waistcoat."

Christopher nearly had an apoplexy on the spot. He drew up short in shock.

To his horror, the other adults in the group clapped and nodded their agreement, as if this heretical redefinition of Polaris had come as a commandment from the Crown.

"And that one?" asked the lady astronomer.

Christopher shook his head and approached with caution. Surely, he had misheard her.

"Yes, that is absolutely the front wheel of a landaulet. And this one?"

He was wrong.

She was a madwoman.

"Very good, Nigel!" She ruffled the woolen

cap of a boy with a gap-toothed grin. "That is obviously the oar of a Viking's wooden vessel."

"It is nothing of the sort," Christopher spluttered as he shouldered his way into the group. "That is Leo Minor, identifiable due to the arrangement of the three stars visible to the naked eye and its northern celestial position between Leo and Ursa Major."

"Impossible," she said without the slightest hesitation. "Nigel just said it was a rowing paddle."

"Nigel," Christopher said, staring down at the apple-cheeked moppet, "is five years old."

"Six," Nigel corrected.

"Six," Christopher agreed. "He is hardly a member of the Royal Astronomical Society."

"There is no Royal Astronomical Society," the lady astronomer pointed out.

"Is that why I'm not a member?" Nigel whispered.

"No one who thinks Polaris is a spangle upon Beau Brummell's waistcoat would qualify," Christopher said. "Gentlemen astronomers are serious, science-minded scholars."

"Nigel isn't a gentleman," she replied. "Neither am I. This is our tour."

"But you must comprehend the difference between 'true' and 'false' information." He jabbed his finger at the sky. "Fact: this is the North Star, not a dandy's spangle. Fact: *that* is Leo Minor, not the oar of some boat."

"Says who?" a little girl with one mitten

piped up. "If there's no Royal Astronomical Society, then you're not a member of it either."

Christopher clenched his teeth to stave off a sharp reply. They were missing the point. Lectures were meant to convey *facts*.

Yet the entire group was staring at him as if *he* were the one who couldn't tell Puppis from Pyxis. Lunatics, all of them.

He could recognize a lost cause. Rather than continue trying to impose reality on people determined to ignore logic, he spun away from the group and stalked back toward the castle.

At least the ridiculous sky-walk only occurred once a month. He'd be long gone before the next round of willful ignorance ensued. And as for the exasperating young lady leading the blind?

He'd take care never to cross paths with her again.

CHAPTER 3

The following morning, Christopher approached the castle's crowded public dining area with trepidation. He hoped the high passions of the previous night would not come back to haunt him. He rolled his eyes at himself for his folly.

Two-and-thirty years without the slightest hint of scandal, only to lose his head over the proper identification of constellations.

He sighed. Not exactly the impression a man wished to give when hoping to attract a wife. He would not be surprised if his name were now synonymous with whatever the male equivalent of "excitable bluestocking spinster" might be. It would serve him right if he were forced to cut his holiday even shorter than he had planned.

All he could do was make the best of it. He rolled back his shoulders and strode straight into the crowded common area, come what may. No matter what the latest gossip might entail, he still needed to break his fast.

"Mr. Pringle," bubbled a breathless female voice. "I don't know if you remember, but on my first day here, you recommended the white sauce for my fish. It turned out to be quite a pleasing combination of—"

"Several of us are working on props tonight for a new play," another young lady interrupted, practically bouncing in place. "If you'd like to stop by the amphitheater—"

"It's snowing," blurted out a different young lady. "A perfect day for a sleigh ride. After we break our fast—"

"Let him eat in peace, all of you," scolded an older matron before treating him to a saucy wink. She lowered her voice and added, "See you in the greenhouse in thirty minutes?"

Christopher didn't answer. There was no opportunity to do so.

In the quarter hour it took him to walk the twenty feet from the dining hall entrance to the first available table, dozens of young women stepped into his path to beg him to accompany them on more activities than he had even realized this tiny village offered.

Some of the invitations were delivered with pink cheeks and a shy stammer. Others' suggestions were so direct Christopher feared his own cheeks were in danger of blushing.

By the time he was finally able to take refuge at a private table, his heart was thudding hard enough to rattle the handkerchief in his waistcoat.

"What is happening?" he whispered to the first footman to pass by with tea and coffee.

"They've been waiting for you for hours, milord." The footman placed sugar on the table for the tea. "Ever since this morning's service."

Sunday. Christopher's jaw dropped in comprehension.

The first banns announcing his brother's betrothal had been read this morning in the local church.

Which made him the newest commodity.

He lifted his steaming cup to his mouth and pretended not to notice the surreptitious female glances being tossed his way.

Was he happy now? His wish had come true. Women were climbing over each other to approach him as if he'd become his rakish brother. But something was different.

Christopher had spent the past fortnight befriending the other guests in the castle. There were very few he didn't recognize by name. None of the introductions had resulted in a love interest... Or much female interest at all. All eyes had been focused on Nick. Until today.

Instead of swooning, as females were wont to do whenever Nick walked into their midst, they were presenting themselves directly to Christopher. There was no need to beg for introductions, because the formalities had already occurred.

He'd spent a lifetime wishing to be in his brother's place. Now that he was suddenly the object of every unwed young lady's attention, he found it more than a bit overwhelming. He accepted toast and kippers from the next footman, but his appetite had vanished.

This was a positive development, he assured himself. The Great Bride Hunt had become exponentially easier. With limitless options, it should take no time at all to find his missing half. Someone sweet and sensible, like-minded and logical, with a hunger to explore the world around them. The perfect partner.

He should start by accepting a few invitations. Perhaps a courtship would blossom from there. He pushed to his feet and stepped into their midst.

"Mr. Pringle," cooed a woman. "I hear you like to stay up all night. So do I."

Another pressed the side of her bosom into his arm. "I get so lost in this big castle. Can you help me find my chamber?"

"When you tire of her," a third woman murmured into his ear, "I can show you things she's never dreamed of."

Christopher's stomach clenched. These women weren't interested in him. They wanted a replacement for their favorite rake. Someone to spend a pleasurable hour with, and never see again. He did not know how to answer.

Just like him, these women were here on holiday. Another man would have been delighted to accept any favors they might offer. But Christopher had no wish to become a copy of his brother. Nor did he wish to repeat the disastrous marriage his parents had suffered. He meant to do *better*. He wanted a match to last for eternity.

"Excuse me, ladies," he murmured. "I've just recalled an engagement elsewhere."

"Until later," they purred. "You know where to find us."

One of the ladies tucked a calling card into Christopher's jacket pocket and whispered, "Directions to my guest chamber are on the other side."

His plan to exit the dining hall posthaste was hampered by a dozen other ladies, begging him to meet them here or there on pretenses ranging from the mundane to nonexistent. By the time he burst out of the dining area, he'd lost count of the number of times he'd been propositioned.

He stalked over to the spiral staircase and hurried up to the sixth floor. How on earth had his brother lived like this? Christopher had wanted the distracting rake out of the picture, not to become Nick's surrogate. Christopher's fingers clenched.

Their sire would have loved this turn of events. Father believed that his ill-fated attempt to limit himself to a single woman was the cause of all the trouble in his life. He had warned his sons never to make the same mistake. *Wed if you must, but keep as many mistresses as you please.* The trick was finding a wife who didn't care, not some shrew who cared too much. Love was a fairy story.

With sermons like that at home, Saint Nick could not help but be their father's favorite. He was living the life their father wanted for himself.

On the other hand, bookish Christopher with his collection of globes and well-used telescope, had never been anything but a disappointment.

Until now. The past hour fending off the amorous advances of beautiful women would have been the first time he made his father proud.

An achievement he no longer wanted.

He banged on his brother's guest chamber door. That he should need advice now after a lifetime of being self-sufficient rankled. But Christopher had never been in this position before. He needed to stop it. If there was an easy way to deflect unwanted attention without hurting feelings, Nick would know.

But he did not answer the knock.

Christopher raked a hand through his hair. His brother must be with his intended. Penelope Mitchell's cottage was only a few hundred feet from the castle. He could be there in no time.

Provided the reception area in front of the exit had not turned into a gauntlet.

He hurried down the steps. As he feared, the public commons that had been all but vacant the night before now brimmed with activity. He lowered the brim of his hat to hide his eyes and dashed through the middle to the exit without looking up or slowing down.

When he arrived at Penelope's house, his brother answered the door.

"How do you stand it?" Christopher slipped inside as if the hounds of hell nipped at his heels. "All the women competing to be the next hash mark on your bedpost?"

"I picked one," Nick said cheerfully. "Technically, I picked the one who used me as a hash mark on *her* bedpost."

"I can hear you," Penelope said as she walked around the corner bearing a plate of fresh-made biscuits. "Good morning, Chris. Come join us by the fire."

Christopher sat on the edge of a sofa and accepted a biscuit.

Penelope handed a stack to Nick, then set the plate next to a pair of glass turtledoves upon the mantel.

"What's wrong?" Nick asked, his brow lining with concern. "Did your trip get canceled?"

Penelope leaned forward. "Are you going somewhere?"

"Chris is always going somewhere," Nick said with a smile. "Help me talk him into coming back at least once a year or we may never see him again."

"I hope to share my journeys with a wife." Christopher lifted the calling card from his jacket pocket and flung it toward his brother. "Not with whoever wrote this."

Nick let out a low whistle when he discovered the handwritten bedchamber directions on the other side. "Brilliant. Who doesn't love a woman who knows her own mind?"

Penelope tossed the calling card straight into the fire. "You were saying?"

"See?" he said. "You know your own mind. I'm smitten." He sniffed at her. "Or maybe it's your perfume."

She shoved him away with a laugh and turned to Christopher. "What are you looking for in a wife?"

"Perfection," Nick answered dryly before Christopher had a chance to reply.

His brother was only half right.

"It isn't just a matter of finding the perfect woman," he said carefully. "I need to be the perfect match for her, too."

Nick's gaze met his and he nodded in understanding.

When their mother had walked away from their unhappy home never to return, she hadn't just left their horrid father. She had tossed aside the entire family.

He could not go through that again.

Only by finding a woman who was a one-hundred-percent match to him in all things could Christopher be certain their union would have a chance.

"You don't want a meaningless affair," Penelope prompted. "You want a woman who…"

"Shares my interests," Christopher said. "That should be a good foundation."

Nick ticked traits off on his fingers. "Unwillingness to put down roots, proclivity toward pedantic fact-checking, improbable command of languages, inability to suffer a mistake in silence, obsession with fact-gathering in order to always be right—"

"You're repeating yourself with different phrasing," Christopher said in irritation.

"I rest my case," his brother murmured. "This is going to be fun."

Penelope waved this aside. "Ignore him. Tell me in your own words."

Christopher thought it over. "I don't think it unreasonable to hope for someone sensible. It's not just a matter of respecting facts and figures. I need someone who can be counted on."

"That's not a wife," Nick said. "That's an abacus."

"Conformity to rules isn't a bad thing," Christopher pointed out. "In a few weeks, you and Penelope are going to make your vows before God. But neither church nor state can *make* you comply. A successful marriage is something two people choose to share."

The amusement faded from his brother's eyes. He understood at once. "We will not repeat their mistakes."

The worst moments of their childhood could be traced back to lack of fidelity. Father had not upheld his vows. Or values of any kind. When Mother left, she broke hers, too. Including the unspoken bonds that should have existed between a mother and her sons.

They had learned all too well the disastrous results of imperfect unions. A perfect match was the only way to ensure a marriage that would last.

"Wanting someone who keeps her word is a perfectly understandable requirement," Penelope said. "Don't worry. I grew up in this town. They're all good people. It won't be hard to find a nice young woman."

"There's too many," Christopher muttered.

Nick stared at him. "What are you talking about? I've seen more women stuffed into Almack's than live in this village."

"Yes, well." Christopher shrugged. "Now that you are taken, they're all throwing themselves at me at once. If I can't locate a good match in the smallest town in England, London will be a thousand times worse."

"Easy." Penelope snuggled against Nick. "You need a matchmaker."

Christopher blinked. "A what?"

"It solves everything at once," she explained. "You won't need to interview every woman in Christmas, because the matchmaker will already know everyone. You need only detail your preferences, and she will find the right bride. You'll be done inside of a week."

Christopher held perfectly still. "I could make a match within a sennight?"

"When is your next trip?" Nick asked.

"Port of London in three weeks." Christopher's chest filled with hope. "I purchased double passage just in case."

"Then 'love of adventure' is a top priority." Penelope smiled at him encouragingly. "Be sure to tell the matchmaker."

Was that truly the best way?

"I don't know." Christopher hesitated. "Involving a third-party…"

"Is often the wisest decision," Penelope finished firmly. "Do you cut your own hair? Extract your own teeth? Tailor your own clothes? When something needs to be done right, an expert is always the right choice."

Christopher let out his breath. "And who is the expert?"

"Miss Gloria Godwin," Penelope said without hesitation. "She lives three cottages to the north. Holly wreath on the front door. You can't miss it."

Nick slanted a look at his bride. "Gloria who believes in love?"

"Of course, Gloria who believes in love." Penelope gave a sharp nod. "She'll make him a match in no time." She turned to Christopher. "Gloria is an absolute darling, and a pillar of the community. She is definitely who you need to see."

The idea was appealing, if unconventional.

"I'll think about it," he said.

"That's a no," Nick whispered. "When Chris gets started thinking about something, he is likely never to stop."

Penelope lifted a finger. "Give me your word you'll stop by as soon as you leave here."

Christopher inclined his head. "Very well. I give my word."

He was not convinced it would work, but it couldn't be worse than what awaited him back at the castle.

"I can send you with a letter of reference." Penelope sat up straight. "Hold on a moment while I fetch some foolscap."

"That won't be necessary." Christopher rose to his feet. "I'm not applying to be a governess. I'm offering to be a client. I'll take it from here."

In fact, there was no reason to waste another moment.

He took his leave from the lovebirds and headed back outside into the lightly falling snow. His boots crunched as he turned north on the snow-packed street and counted out the cottages. The third one bore a holly wreath exactly as Penelope had described.

He presented himself on the doorstep and rapped sharply upon the knocker.

A ruddy-cheeked maid with laughter lines and a streak of gray hair answered the door.

He presented his calling card. "Mr. Christopher Pringle to see Miss Gloria Godwin, if you'd be so kind as to let her know."

The maid frowned over his shoulder at the falling snow, then motioned him inside.

He stepped into the entryway, which opened into a cozy parlor. A coatrack stood to one side. Christopher did not use it.

The maid closed the door behind him. "A moment, please, while I present your card."

Unfortunately for all parties involved, the presenting of the card turned out to be an unnecessary step.

Miss Gloria Godwin herself hurried toward the drawing room, likely in response to the knock. Her obvious consternation upon recognizing the caller might have been humorous if Christopher hadn't felt precisely the same dismay.

The young lady standing before him was none other than the gravy-for-brains madwoman spouting nonsense about dukes and waistcoat spangles in the sky to a group of children and would-be stargazers.

"You have to be bamming me," he muttered beneath his breath.

"I could say the same," she answered hotly, brown eyes flashing. "What the devil are you doing here?"

An excellent question. Christopher would leave at once if he hadn't been forced to give his word.

He thought back. What precisely had he promised? Only that he would stop by? Here he was. Word kept. Game over.

He reached for the door. "I'll see myself out."

"But why are you here?" Miss Godwin shoved delicate fists onto curvy hips and speared him with a frosty glare.

Unbelievable.

He drew himself up to his full height. He had not behaved as a gentleman ought, but nor had he been spreading willful ignorance to impressionable individuals. If he owed her an apology, she owed a bigger one to every poor fool on that tour.

He could not be sorry for attempting to correct her outright lies, but in the name of politesse…

"I apologize for causing a scene," he said magnanimously, "just as I am certain you are sorry for spreading"—horrific, blatant, outlandish—"misinformation."

She folded her arms beneath her breasts. "I'm not sorry."

He scowled at her.

She scowled back.

"Neither am I," he admitted. They might as well be honest. "Astronomy is a serious field. Scholars spend their lifetimes refining the known, and working hard to discover—"

A knock sounded from outside.

"If you please," murmured the maid.

He stepped out of her way.

She creaked open the door and stuck her arm through the crack. Moments later, the door once again closed tight, and a folded square of parchment rested in the maid's hand.

She turned to her mistress. "Note from Miss Mitchell."

It was all Christopher could do not to close his eyes and allow the back of his head to bang against the wall. Repeatedly.

His "letter of reference" had arrived right on time.

Miss Godwin broke the drop of wax and flipped open the message. Half a breath later, her incredulous gaze rose to meet his. "This is absurd."

"I agree," he said fervently. Now they could be done. "As we are in agreement—"

"I'll do it," she said, with all the joy of an impending trip to the hangman's noose. "Not for you, but as a favor to Penelope."

He stared at her in disbelief. "What?"

She sighed. "Consider your apology accepted. Sit down. Madge will watch over us to ensure propriety."

The maid immediately sat at the edge of the closest wingback chair.

Miss Godwin settled herself in the center of a two-person sofa, as though to ensure Christopher would make no attempt to draw near.

She needn't have worried. He was still debating whether to run screaming into the street.

He glanced about the small parlor and chose the wingback chair beside two tall bookcases. Like the maid, he did not settle back against the pillow. He would not be here long.

"I see you like to read," he said, searching for common ground. "I, too, enjoy—"

"You see a collection of books. That doesn't mean they're mine, or that I read them." She arched a brow. "We are not friends. I'm your matchmaker. What do you want in a match?"

He clenched his jaw. Definitely not anyone like her.

Black hair, dark eyes, pink lips, tapered curves... A day ago, he might have considered the combination one of his favorites. Today, he'd rather subject himself to a lifetime of never-ending bachelorhood than end up with a wife bearing anything in common with Miss Godwin.

"Too difficult a question?" she asked with saccharine politeness. "Then let's start with you. What are your credentials?"

Fine. He was going to have to talk to her.

Christopher cleared his throat. "As you may have surmised, I am something of a gentleman astronomer—"

"We are looking for reasons a woman would *want* to wed you," she interrupted sweetly. "Surely there must be something?"

He ground his jaw. "One or two details may fit your requirements. I come from well-respected lineage. I'm currently second in line to a dukedom. Financial stability need not be a concern for my future wife."

She leaned back into the sofa. "Younger brother to an heir presumptive means neither of you are particularly likely to become the next Duke of Silkridge."

He glared at her. If she already knew his family history, why bother to ask?

"Nonetheless…" She tilted her head. "Most of my neighbors have no connections at all. To certain ladies, yours will be attractive indeed."

"I don't want them," he said without thinking, then immediately regretted the outburst.

She scoffed. "Why ever not? One might say that wealth and connections are a potential suitor's two greatest aspects."

One might also say that Beau Brummell's waistcoat is one of the constellations.

And one would be wrong.

He swallowed the terse reply. Miss Godwin was not alone in judging a man solely on the material benefits he could provide. It was best to set proper expectations.

"I am not seeking a perfect bride," he said quietly, "nor do I pretend to be a perfect groom. I am looking for a perfect *match*. Puzzle pieces that fit together. Two halves of a whole, whatever form that might take."

The skepticism fell away from her expression. She gave him a closer look.

"That's… impressively romantic," she admitted. "I take it back. You may catch more women with that angle than your connections to a dukedom."

He shook his head. "I'm not looking for 'women.' I want a marriage that will last forever."

"Don't we all," she murmured, staring down at Penelope's note in her lap. With a start, Miss Godwin crumpled the paper and tossed it into the fire. "I hate letters."

Christopher resolved never to write her one.

"If you had to pick a single characteristic," she said slowly. "A quirk, a personality trait, a hobby. What is the one thing your prospective bride must have?"

"Willingness to travel," he said at once. "It is my greatest passion, and one I very much look forward to sharing with my wife."

From the aghast expression on Miss Godwin's face, he might as well have admitted to a propensity for eating earthworms in clotted cream.

"You don't like travel?" he said in surprise.

"Or travelers," she said briskly. "But matchmaking isn't about me. We have a good base. Come back tomorrow afternoon and I'll introduce you to your first possibility."

"Thank you." He stood but then hesitated, unsure if he was meant to bow, or shake on the deal, or promise to never write letters from abroad. She made no sign.

At last, he decided on simply showing himself to the door.

When he turned around, however, he came face to face with the bookshelves he'd admired upon entering the drawing room. To his surprise, the top two shelves were filled with tomes on astronomy.

"You were telling the truth," he said in shock. "These are perfectly serviceable resources on the venerable field of astronomy, and you haven't read a single page."

She lifted her chin. "I see what I see."

"There are facts in there." He pointed at the spines. "Facts one cannot override with flights of fancy. Constellations have predetermined names."

She arched a brow. "Let me see if my female mind can grasp your logic. Are you attempting to bully me into adopting complete fiction that someone *else* made up, rather than use stories from my own imagination?"

Yes. Yes, that was exactly what he was trying

to do. All parties using the same, agreed-upon designations was how the concept of constellations *worked*.

Yet this was clearly not an argument he had any hope to win. Best to make a quick escape.

"Oh, will you look at the time." He pulled out his pocket watch. "It's…"

Broken.

He gave the pocket watch a frustrated shake. No matter how often he wound the bloody thing, within an hour or two it ceased to function.

Miss Godwin sighed and held out her palm. "Let me see it."

"No need," he said quickly. "I'll find a jeweler who knows how to—"

"Madge?" Miss Godwin pointed her open palm in the direction of her maid.

The maid immediately pulled a small pouch from her apron and pitched it in her mistress's direction with a perfect arc.

Miss Godwin caught the satchel with one hand, sprang to her feet, and snatched Christopher's pocket watch from his fingers.

"Er," he said. "Should I unhook it from my waistcoat, or…"

Using a few small tools from the pouch, Miss Godwin popped the protective backing from his most expensive watch and began poking at the gears within. Christopher's flesh ran cold.

"Hand," she commanded.

Christopher jerked his gaze toward her. "What?"

Madge materialized beside them, a clean handkerchief covering her palm.

Miss Godwin dumped the inner workings of Christopher's favorite pocket watch into the maid's outstretched hand.

One by one, she cleaned each piece with the corner of the handkerchief and nudged it carefully into place. When she finished, she snapped the backing on tight and turned the watch face right-side-up.

A familiar ticking indicated the gears were once again in motion.

Miss Godwin dropped the tools back inside the little bag and tossed the pouch to her maid.

"Now that your timepiece works," she said as if Christopher's mind wasn't exploding like the gears of a broken pocket watch, "Come back tomorrow at two o'clock. I'll introduce you to a sweet, intelligent woman not afraid to travel. Possibly even with you."

Christopher nodded automatically. But as he turned to the door, he suspected he might be more interested in the future surprises Miss Godwin might bring.

CHAPTER 4

*G*loria grimaced at her uninspiring reflection in the looking-glass. "Why are we doing this again?"

"You are matchmaking Mr. Pringle because you promised Miss Mitchell." Madge poked another pin into Gloria's unruly locks. "And I am attempting to tame your hair because you begged me to."

Two stupid decisions in a row. Gloria should just go back to bed.

There was absolutely no reason to primp. She was bound to meet the right man someday, but Mr. Pringle clearly was not that man. She would just have to keep looking.

Besides, as matchmaker, her role was to attract her handsome client to someone else. Not that Mr. Pringle had shown any signs of "love at first sight" with Gloria. Or any sight.

The first time he'd laid eyes on her, he had looked right through her without seeing her at all. The second time, he had been so appalled at how she ran her Saturday evening sky-walks that she doubted her appearance registered at all. And the third time they'd crossed paths... had been because he hoped she could help him marry someone else.

"I'm a henwitted fool," she muttered.

"As you say, ma'am," Madge murmured.

Gloria glared at her maid in the looking-glass. "I don't pay you to agree with me."

"Yes, you do." She stuck another pin into Gloria's hair. "I'm not surprised you forgot how this relationship works, you being a henwitted fool and all."

Gloria burst out laughing.

Madge was the one constant in her life. As much an older sister as a maid, Gloria could not recall a time before Madge. They'd been through so much.

Because she cherished her like a sister, Gloria had offered a healthy severance if Madge preferred to seek a different future. But she had refused to leave Gloria until her mistress was happily married.

Neither of them had thought it would take this long.

"A little harsh on him yesterday, weren't you?" Madge asked as she twisted another curl.

Gloria slanted her a look. "He was harsh first. Preaching 'one true constellation' at me on two separate occasions. Explaining things I already know. Both presumptuous and insulting. I cannot be expected to smile and nod."

"All men expect women to smile and nod."

"Then I am doomed to spinsterhood." Not true. Gloria would never stop believing the right man was out there somewhere. She just wished a tiny part of her wasn't dying to impress Mr. Wrong One. "Besides, we're trying to marry him off."

"I'm not trying anything." Madge teased out a curl. "I'm impartial."

Gloria chuckled. "You've never once been impartial."

"Hold still," Madge scolded. "You'll ruin your hair."

Gloria wrinkled her nose. "Isn't a French twist a little too obvious?"

"It's attractive," Madge said.

"I'm not trying to attract him," Gloria insisted. "I just don't want to look frumpy next to Désirée."

"Everyone looks frumpy next to Mademoiselle le Duc," Madge pointed out. "Chandeliers look frumpy. Constellations look frumpy. No matter what names they bear."

"You're not helping," Gloria muttered.

Madge lifted a shoulder. "Perhaps he'll fall head over heels and be out of your life for good. Isn't that what you want?"

"Yes," Gloria said firmly. "That's exactly what I want. The sooner he chooses a bride, the sooner we can all move on."

The sooner she'd find happiness of her own.

Madge slipped the final pin into Gloria's hair. "And you think Mademoiselle le Duc will please him?"

"Désirée makes chandeliers look frumpy," Gloria said with a sigh. "Of course she'll do."

It was more than a matter of matching his list of wants with the right woman. If she could find him a twin soul, there would be no stopping true love from blossoming. Désirée was a good start.

Mr. Pringle had not mentioned beauty as a prerequisite, but Gloria doubted he was opposed to the trait. Besides, his priority was willingness to travel. Désirée had come from France years ago.

Granted, her family had been fleeing execution. The French Revolution had severely curtailed life expectancy for any nationals connected to the aristocracy. This village was about as far from the battlefield as one could get.

More to the point, England was not the le Duc family's first trip. Prior to becoming refugees, they had lived lives of splendor that included luxurious holidays in unusual places. Désirée would get on splendidly with Mr. Pringle.

Gloria made her way to the front parlor and ran her finger along her shelves. Adventure was not for her. She preferred to do her traveling via the pages of the book. It was easier. Safer.

She knelt below the row of the astronomy tomes to her collection of travel journals. She selected one on France and thumbed through the pages to refresh her memory of the details. Her role might not be to take part in her client's conversation, but she did not wish to seem a country greenhorn in comparison.

When the knock came, she shoved the travel volume back in its home and motioned for Madge to open the door.

Had Gloria thought she put extra attention to her appearance this morning? Christopher Pringle looked positively divine.

His dark hair was carefully unkempt in the current style. His neckcloth folded to the perfect balance between decorative and unassuming. A well-cut coat of blue superfine brought out the contours of his shoulders. The buttery-soft buckskins encasing his strong legs… Well.

Désirée was going to love him.

"Two o'clock." He lifted a still-functioning pocket watch from inside his jacket. "Magnificent work."

How fortunate that she'd wasted an hour on her hair. She hadn't rated a second glance. He cared more about his watch.

She snatched her bonnet from the sofa and smashed it on to her head. "Let's go. It is a bit of a walk, but the sun is out and—"

"I brought a carriage." He beamed at her.

She blinked at him. "You brought a what?"

"A chariot, to be exact. We'll ride over." He offered her his elbow. "Ready?"

"You brought a chariot to save yourself a walk of five hundred feet?"

He gestured at the carriage behind him. "I wanted to make a good impression."

It was a beautiful carriage.

Gloria hated it.

"Do you want her to be interested in you or your chariot?" she asked flatly.

His eyes sparkled. "We have to travel somehow, don't we?"

Gloria was about to retort that her legs worked quite well, thank you very much, when she realized "we" wasn't referring to her at all.

He meant he and his future wife would spend big portions of their lives on travel adventures. He would not wish to arrive on foot and have a potential bride think for a moment that holidays with him would be spent jostling for room atop a crowded mail coach.

She ignored his proffered elbow. He was only being polite. She didn't need his help.

"Come along, Madge," she called over her shoulder. "We are traveling by chariot today."

Unlike a barouche or a landau, Mr. Pringle's chariot featured two forward-facing benches. Gloria and Mr. Pringle took the front seats, and Madge settled in behind them.

"Where to?" Mr. Pringle asked.

Gloria pointed. "We'll take the first left up ahead."

"Thank you for doing this." His eyes were warm, his smile sincere. "I had begun to think I was running out of time."

She blinked. "How could you possibly be running out of time? You cannot be more than what, nine-and-twenty?"

"Two-and-thirty," he answered. "But I was referring to my time in Christmas coming to a close. I'm here for a month, and a fortnight is already gone."

Betrothed and wed in two weeks' time? That wasn't cutting things close. That was impossible.

"Do you plan to kidnap a wife?" she asked. "What about banns? They take three weeks to read."

"I'll get a special license if necessary," he said as if private audiences with the Archbishop of Canterbury were as easy to procure as penny pies. "Then sweep my bride off on a magnificent adventure."

Gloria could not imagine a worse proposal. If some suitor threatened to upend her from everything familiar, she would slam the door in his face.

She rather suspected Désirée le Duc would not have the same reaction.

"Then let's get started." Gloria motioned toward the horses and tried not to feel as though she was missing out. "With luck, the first meeting will be the charm."

Désirée would be a very lucky woman. Christopher Pringle was wealthy, well-connected, and handsome. More than that, he didn't seek a wife, but a love match. He wanted a marriage that would last forever. What woman could resist?

"Do you travel often?" he asked.

"Never," she answered without hesitation.

"Never?" he repeated in horror. "You just stay… *here?*"

"I like Christmas," she said tightly. "I know

what to expect in every corner, and every season."

He cast a doubtful look at the piles of snow on both sides of the road. "Is there more than one season?"

"No," she answered cheerfully. "It brings me comfort when there are no surprises."

"Surprises are good," he insisted. "Some would say surprises are the entire point of travel."

"I would never say such a thing," she assured him.

His brow furrowed. "There's so much world out there. I cannot imagine voluntarily limiting myself to a minuscule part."

Gloria lifted her chin. They could not be more incompatible.

She could not care if she failed to live up to his standards, or if he judged her for choosing to stay close to home. She had no wish to go anywhere else, and even less inclination to risk her heart with someone who would.

"Have you never been on a boat?" he asked.

Her chest seized at the thought. "Boats can sink."

He arched a brow. "How often does that happen?"

She tried to breathe as her pulse pounded in her ears. "More often than you think."

He frowned. "But if you've never—"

Madge cleared her throat.

Gloria started. There was only one road, and they'd almost missed their turn.

"Here." She pointed to the right.

His face brightened. "The le Duc residence?"

Her stomach sank. "You know it?"

"I stopped by on my way in." He patted the squab. "This is where I rented my chariot. I didn't realize the le Duc siblings had a sister."

Gloria stared at the chariot.

Of course he hadn't driven up from London in such a small conveyance. For a month-long holiday hundreds of miles away, he would have needed a stately coach, a driver, a valet, trunks of clothing.

He spun to face her. "Can we tour their smithy?"

"No, we cannot tour the smithy," she shushed him. "We are not here to do man things, we're here to meet women."

Madge's cough sounded suspiciously like, *Also a man thing*.

Gloria ignored her. They were here on business. With luck, Cupid would show up to the meeting.

She found it best not to inform people they were being matchmade so the note she had sent round to Désirée only mentioned she would stop by before teatime with a friend.

The butler ushered them into a beautiful entryway.

If Désirée was surprised that the friend in question was the exceptionally handsome brother of the equally handsome rake who had turned their town on its ear, she made no sign.

Either she had always suspected that Gloria

hobnobbed with attractive heirs to dukedoms, or Désirée possessed a particularly impressive poker face.

"Allow me to present Mr. Christopher Pringle." Gloria turned to her client. "Mr. Pringle, this is Mademoiselle le Duc."

"Enchanté," he murmured. Rather than bow or even press his lips to her fingers, they leaned forward and exchanged air kisses on both sides of their cheeks.

"It is exactly like being in France," Désirée said in her charming accent, with an equally charming giggle. "Do you speak French, Monsieur Pringle?"

Those were the last words Gloria understood for the next quarter hour.

She followed them into a lush drawing room, joined them before the fire, accepted tea when Désirée served it, and pretended to follow along.

One did not need to speak French to understand what was happening: Love at first sight, right before her eyes. Gloria was the greatest matchmaker in the history of matchmakers. Scant moments into the first introduction, and these two were already carrying on as if they'd known each other their entire lives.

She did her best to look pleased, rather than put out. Mr. Pringle was being charming, and Désirée was a treasure. They did not mean to exclude her. They likely hadn't realized she wasn't following along with what appeared to be rapid-fire flirty little jokes.

Gloria doubted that Désirée had much opportunity to speak French outside of her family, so it must be a relief to feel eloquent and witty again instead of tongue-tied and foreign. Whatever she was saying now had him chuckling in commiseration over some shared experience or another.

If there was a difference between Désirée's French accent and Mr. Pringle's, Gloria could not discern it. Either he'd had the best French tutors in all of England, or he'd spent a significant amount of time in France. No wonder he and Désirée had so much to discuss.

Gloria reminded herself it was not the matchmaker's place to horn in. No matter how intrigued she was by their budding romance... and whatever they were saying in French.

She owned no less than three travel journals about France, one dedicated entirely to Paris. The illustrations were magnificent but could not hold a candle to the true experience. Yet it would have to be enough.

Her arms hugged tighter about her chest. No matter how much she longed to see places like Paris with her own eyes, the thought of traveling there filled her with such panic it squeezed the air from her lungs.

Only a dunce would go in this climate. The war was ongoing, with more atrocities reported every day. She would stay right here in Christmas, thank you very much. The safest corner in all of England.

Désirée's tinkling laugh rang out yet again, and she patted Gloria's arm in delight. "It is marvelous that you bring your friend to me. For so much time, I only speak French with my brothers."

Mr. Pringle leaned back in surprise. "Surely many of the well-appointed tourists have had a French lesson or two?"

"Yes, yes, they have lessons." Désirée wrinkled her nose. "But they think all French people are from Paris. They do not know my village as you do."

Gloria blinked. He had visited the exact village? Could there possibly be a better sign?

"It is now many years, and I am still an outsider." Her expression was wistful. "Some of the neighbors, they see us as a caricature, and not a welcome one."

Gloria's stomach twisted. She liked to believe that her bighearted town would welcome anyone needing a safe place to stay, just as in the Christmas story, and she hated to think her home had made anyone feel unwelcome.

Yet she was not naïve. England was at war. Caricatures of the French appeared in every newspaper. The words people used when describing Désirée's homeland were unkind, to say the least.

Gloria touched her fingertips to her friend's arm. "Christmas is open to everyone. I'm glad you're here. If there's ever anything I can do…"

Désirée smiled. "You are always sweet, and a good friend. Do not worry. You bring gentlemen like Monsieur Pringle, of course I am fine."

He grinned back at her, then pulled a face

when he glimpsed the hour on the clock next to the window. "Do the French observe the custom of afternoon visits lasting no more than twenty or thirty minutes?"

She made a pretty moue. "I do not know the regulations. You may stay as long as you please."

He should and would. Gloria was a brilliant matchmaker. Excellent work. She should go home, bake herself a cake, eat the whole thing.

"It's best we follow protocol. I wouldn't wish to add unnecessary scandal to your troubles." He added something in French that turned Désirée's cheeks pink.

"Come back soon," she said with a laugh. "Both of you."

They bid their leave and climbed back into the carriage. Soon they were back on the road.

Gloria did not bother to ask how the meeting had gone. The answer was obvious. *C'est l'amour.*

Gloria was thrilled at Désirée's positive reception. Mostly thrilled. Only an unprofessional matchmaker would feel a tiny pinch of envy.

She sent Mr. Pringle a covert glance from the corner of her eye.

She needed a man that was his complete opposite. He was adventurous, fearless, worldly. Gloria didn't require any of that. It made him dangerous. Besides, he was a client.

Well, an ex-client. He'd found his future Madame Pringle in the space of an hour.

"Come along, Madge," she said the moment

the wheels of the chariot came to a stop before her house. "Let's not keep Mr. Pringle."

She scrambled down without waiting for his aid and hurried back inside her cottage. She tossed her bonnet on the chair beside the adventure books and kept on walking past the kitchen, past her private observatory, and into her bedchamber.

She came to a stop in front of the old wooden trunk and flipped up the lid.

"Paris," Madge said behind her. "Last time you packed it, it was for Paris."

"I've changed my mind." Gloria began yanking items from the trunk. "That was weeks ago."

Madge opened the armoire. "Where are we going now?"

"Venice," Gloria said decisively. "We will have pasta at an outdoor café and spend the afternoon in a private gondola."

Madge nodded. "I'll pack the parasols. It is important to protect oneself from the elements."

No matter how many times they played this game, packing a trunk for a holiday they would never take, Madge had not once asked why Gloria bothered.

She didn't have to. She had been there when Gloria's faith in adventure had been destroyed.

Six years ago, Gloria had experienced her one and only London season. It had been a smashing success. She'd been betrothed by her fifth ball. When her suitor set off to make his fortune and never came home, Father had told her not to worry. She was still young. There was plenty of time.

Father *always* said not to worry.

He was an experienced Navy Captain. He never worried about anything. He taught Gloria the stars so that she could learn to navigate as well as he could. Then he sailed off to war. That was the last she saw him.

The Crown provided handsomely in such cases. Gloria did not want money. She wanted her father. And Mother… never recovered. Laudanum was the only thing that got her through the night, until one morning she didn't wake up at all.

And then Gloria was alone.

So, no. She would not be traveling. Or entrusting her heart to anyone who did. All it could lead to was grief and loss.

With a sigh, she closed the lid on her trunk and locked her dreams inside.

CHAPTER 5

*G*loria shoved a hunk of hair out of her eyes and replaced the final fastening on her orrery. This time, when she activated the mechanism, the tiny solar system rotated the planets without a strange grinding sound every time Venus passed Mars.

Flushed with satisfaction, she pushed to her feet and brushed the wrinkles from her skirts. Or tried to. As usual, her wrinkle situation was hopeless. Not that it mattered. She was in a comfortable old housedress in her comfortable old house tinkering with her comfortable old orrery. Things were exactly as they should be.

Her next sky-walk wasn't for another month. Mr. Pringle was off signing a bilingual wedding contract. Gloria did not have to take a single step out of her cottage if she didn't wish to.

Complete freedom.

She could play with her orrery all afternoon, reread her adventure books all evening, peer up at the stars all night… Anything she wished.

Gloria switched off her orrery and sighed. None of her favorite things sounded fun today. They sounded lonely.

What she needed was something to take her mind off how long it was taking for Prince Wonderful to find her. It would happen when the time was right. In the meantime...

She headed straight to the kitchen.

Madge was already waiting. "Plum pudding?"

"Plum pudding," Gloria agreed.

Madge hauled the framed recipe from the wall, ran an unnecessary dust rag across its pristine glass surface, and propped it in a place of honor in the center of the prepping table.

Neither of them would be giving it another look. This was tradition. Gloria had memorized her mother's careful hand the very first day she'd been allowed to help with the process.

The wonderful thing about Christmas pudding, Mother had explained, was that one was not obliged to wait for Christmas. The high quantity of liquor it contained meant a good pudding could be prepared up to a year or more before it was consumed. Wasn't that indeed a cause for high spirits?

Gloria smiled at the memory. She washed all traces of the orrery from her hands and dried them on a clean cloth. "Ready?"

"Ready." Madge began pulling dried fruits from the cupboard and placing them onto the prepping table.

Gloria sorted them into piles.

Plum pudding was a tradition the entire family had enjoyed. When Father sailed off, Mother and Gloria would immediately begin a new batch. When he returned, they would all enjoy it together.

Mother considered it a good luck charm. Every day, she would pass by the hook where the dried pudding hung and touch her fingertips to the cloth to wish her husband Godspeed.

Gloria had learned to do the same.

Although her parents were gone, making the pudding let her feel connected to her family again. As if her mother's gay laughter still rang through the kitchen as she tossed any spices on hand into the mix with merry abandon.

As if Father were still a mere *Godspeed* away. As if family could walk through the door at any moment.

The knocker banged against its brass base.

Gloria jumped and sent a startled glance toward her maid.

Madge hurried to the door and flung it open wide.

Christopher Pringle swept in, a slight frown of confusion upon his handsome face. "Why does your cottage smell like nutmeg and brandy?"

Gloria's chest gave an erratic flutter.

"Miss Godwin is making pudding," replied Madge, the traitor. "The kitchen is that way."

It didn't matter. He'd already witnessed her tearing about the corner like a child awaiting a visit from the Three Kings. Gloria's cheeks heated in mortification.

She straightened her spine. It was the only choice. There was no hope of straightening her wild hair or her wrinkled gown.

"What are you doing here?" she asked.

"Am I too early?" He flinched in chagrin. "We did not set a time, but yesterday you preferred two o'clock in the afternoon, so I assumed…"

Gloria tried to understand what he was saying. "You still want me to matchmake you?"

His frown grew deeper. "Isn't that what we agreed to?"

"I thought we finished," she stammered.

He tilted his head. "You expect all your clients to fall in love at first sight?"

When introduced to Désirée? Why, yes. Gloria did. They had seemed perfect together.

She tried to understand. "You didn't like Mademoiselle le Duc?"

"She's sweet and beautiful and charming," he said. "And not what I'm looking for."

"You want rude and unkempt and prickly?" Gloria asked doubtfully. "Perhaps you should have mentioned those requirements from the start."

"Charm and beauty are perfectly acceptable traits," he assured her. "But when I said willingness to travel, I had something else in mind."

"The pudding," Madge whispered. "If we leave it unattended, it'll…"

Gloria sent her a flat look. Absolutely nothing would happen to the pudding. But

Madge knew Gloria hated the idea of leaving it unfinished.

"Come with me," she said to Mr. Pringle. "You may explain your revised demands as I finish in the kitchen."

Mr. Pringle placed his hat on the rack and strode forward.

Madge immediately busied herself straightening the cushions on the far side of the parlor.

"You too, Madge," Gloria said in warning. "Propriety."

They traipsed into the kitchen as one.

Gloria reached for an apron. It was a strange feeling to have three people in the kitchen again. Familiar and unsettling.

He took in the disarray of ingredients spread over the prepping table. "You're making a pudding?"

She pointed at the framed directions propped beside the bottle of brandy. "My mother's family recipe."

He stepped closer to investigate.

Gloria dumped dried fruits into a large bowl of suet. "What was wrong with Mademoiselle le Duc?"

"Nothing," he said. "She was as well-traveled as you described. But she has been too long without her homeland. The moment war is over, she wishes to return and never leave."

"I see," Gloria said and reached for an egg. "Let me think of someone with more current desire to travel."

He stepped closer. "I am not certain adven-

ture is my top priority after all. I was thinking…
What are you doing with that egg?"

She cracked it against the bowl and dumped the contents inside. "Adding it to the mix."

"You didn't measure the fruit. The recipe clearly explains the ratio of egg to dried fruits, and I watched you dump them in willy-nilly." He pointed across the prepping table. "Have you read the recipe you're using?"

Gloria grinned and reached for another egg.

Ignoring the recipe was part of the tradition. Each time Father sailed off, they started a pudding with whatever they found in the pantry.

Imagination was more important than memorization, Mother always said. They would place their foreheads together and imagine how happy they would all be when it was time to taste the pudding. No matter how it turned out.

"I'll fetch another apron," Madge said, and slipped out of the kitchen.

Gloria doubted Mr. Pringle had that much interest in her family pudding.

"If not a travel partner," she said as she dumped another egg into the bowl, "what is your new priority?"

"Helping you with this pudding," he said without hesitation. "I think we should start over. How much suet do you have? According to the recipe—"

"I cannot find your match if you don't tell me what you want," she reminded him.

"Nutmeg isn't next," he said as he watched her grate its essence over the bowl. "This is *your* family recipe. First comes treacle or molasses, and then ginger, cinnamon, and—"

He reached for the bowl.

She spun it off the counter and out of his grasp.

He stepped forward, trapping her with her back to the table and only a wobbly bowl of pudding between them.

He reached out his hands, as if to rescue the bowl. Or to cover her trembling hands with his for support. His dark eyes were so close to hers.

"The spices…" he said hoarsely.

"I'm wild," she whispered without moving a muscle. "You can't stop me."

His gaze lowered to her mouth.

Breathing was suddenly difficult. She tried not to lick her lips. The smell of the brandy must be going to her head.

His gaze lowered even more, from her parted lips down to the bowl of sloppy pudding resting dangerously close to his starched white cravat.

He jumped away as if its proximity had scalded him.

"My apologies," he said quickly. "Recipes exist for a reason. I tend to lose my head when rules aren't attended to. It is a personality flaw."

Part of her wished he'd lost his head just a few moments longer.

"Is that what you want?" she asked when she found her voice. "Someone who prefers facts to adventure?"

He turned to face her in surprise. "Travels *are*

about facts. One can read as many secondhand journals as one wishes, but nothing compares to a first-hand fact-finding mission."

She stared at him. "You think of exotic holidays in far-flung places as research opportunities?"

"Doesn't everyone?" he asked.

"No," she said.

"Why do explorers explore?" he asked. "Because they're searching for something."

"Searching for facts," she said doubtfully.

"Of course. What are travel journals, if not a record of information gathered during a reconnaissance mission?" His eyes lit up. "Geography, weather patterns, the rules and customs of local traditions…"

Rules again.

"I suppose that explains your ability with French. To you, it's nothing more than a set of rules to follow?"

"Everything has a right way," he said. "That's what I strive for. In life, and in marriage. My ideal bride will also have the ability to analyze the world around her and behave accordingly."

"Someone who doesn't change," she said. "Someone obsessed with random facts, who over-analyzes how everything works. I know just the woman."

He brightened. "You do?"

Gloria handed the pudding bowl to Madge and took off the apron. "Just a short walk away."

"I brought my carriage."

"You needn't try to impress her with material

things." Gloria wrapped her longest pelisse about her wrinkled dress and tied a bonnet over her tangled hair. "Toss out some obscure facts, and she shall swoon at your feet."

Gloria certainly would not be.

Mr. Pringle had no imagination. If there was one trait she prized above all others, it was the ability to let the world go and just be silly once in a while. If only from inside the safety of one's own mind.

When they arrived at the castle, he shot her a look of surprise. "Here? Where are we going?"

"We'll try the aviary first."

He wanted someone knowledgeable—nay, passionate—about obscure facts? No one fit that bill better than Miss Virginia Underwood.

When they entered the aviary, she was standing next to a pear tree tossing grain to a partridge.

At the sound of the door, Virginia glanced up from her task. "A rose by any other name may smell as sweet, but a well-fed partridge prefers to dine upon dandelions."

The moment of truth. Gloria sent a nervous glance toward Mr. Pringle.

An answering grin already spread across his handsome face. "How are Dasher and Dancer?"

"Dasher's wing is mending nicely," Virginia replied with satisfaction. "She'll be flying again in no time."

Gloria faltered. "You already know each other?"

Virginia's eyes turned dreamy. "He showed me the stars once."

A ludicrous stab of envy streaked inside of Gloria's chest. They didn't just know each other. They had shared a romantic evening. Two fact-obsessed souls joined beneath the stars.

Her stomach soured. "When was this?"

"A week or so ago?" Mr. Pringle guessed, then turned to Virginia. "Do you recall the date?"

She nodded. "A doodlebug's hole gets ever larger during a waxing moon."

Gloria steadied her breath. There was no reason to be vexed. She had specifically brought Mr. Pringle here to matchmake him with Virginia. If they'd already had a head start, it only made her job easier.

To give them privacy, Gloria drifted away and tried not to pay attention.

For a matchmaker, her recent history with men was appallingly blank. She didn't need the conversation to be in French to feel excluded. She watched in silence as they laughed over some shared remembrance she had not been a part of.

Someday, the right man would sweep into her life, fall in love, and spend the rest of their days—

"—much like trout chasing each other to the waterfall." Virginia turned to Gloria. "You should try it."

Try what? Gloria blinked. Perhaps she ought to have been paying attention.

"I don't chase waterfalls," she stammered. "I'm not a trout."

"How about rivers and lakes?" Virginia insisted. "We have those. You used to love ice-skating."

Mr. Pringle's eyes lit up. "Christmas has a skating pond?"

Virginia nodded. "Frozen over almost year-round. Gloria knows it."

Gloria did know it. Her father had taught her to swim in those frigid waters, during one of the few months without ice.

Virginia was right. Gloria used to love the water. Before it had caused her to lose everyone she had ever loved. Her throat grew thick at the memory.

Mr. Pringle grinned. "We should all go."

"No," she said flatly.

His brows furrowed. "But Virginia said—"

"You should go with her," Gloria said firmly. "I'll keep my feet on dry land, if you please."

"And your head tilted toward the stars," Virginia added. "Take care not to focus so much on the sky that you fail to live your life on earth."

Mr. Pringle cocked his head. "Is that an Icarus reference?"

"It's a Gloria reference," Virginia said. "She forgets that water is life."

Gloria crossed her arms. Water was not life. Water was death.

"I love the water," Mr. Pringle agreed. "Have you been to the canals of Venice?"

Gloria made a mental note to unpack her

trunk the moment she returned home. She had to stop picking places that reminded her of him.

Virginia raised her brows with interest. "Is there anywhere you haven't been?"

His gaze sparkled. "I dream of visiting India."

Gloria's stomach roiled at the thought.

"How coincidental." Virginia's eyes widened. "Gloria—"

"—has nothing to do with India," Gloria finished firmly.

The men she was interested in... Now, that was another story. She'd come *so* close to happy ever after before it had slipped away. All because of India.

"The beautiful colors, the gorgeous weather, the scent of the spice bazaars..." Mr. Pringle was saying. "It must be paradise."

Indeed. Gloria's one and only suitor had set off for the subcontinent as an officer in the East India Company. He was to make his fortune, then come back for Gloria, and they would live happily ever after.

By his third letter home, it was obvious he liked *there* better than *here*. Before long, the letters stopped coming altogether.

A shared future with her had paled next to the promise of adventure.

"Have you any ties to the East India Company?" Virginia asked Mr. Pringle.

Gloria sent her a bloodcurdling scowl.

"No, thank heavens." He laughed. "I needn't worry about only going where the Company sends me. I can stay as long as I please."

Exactly the problem. Gloria swallowed. She hoped his dream of India remained just that—a dream. Once he sailed off, he would never be back. Either because he chose not to return...

Or because the ocean wouldn't allow it.

CHAPTER 6

*T*he following day, Christopher regretted taking his nuncheon with his brother and soon-to-be sister-in-law. Their only interest was in the matchmaking process. Penelope's insights were relentlessly scientific. And Nick's comments were relentlessly... Nick.

"Maybe you *should* marry Virginia," he said without bothering to hide his amusement. "You're an odd duck, she likes birds... Match made in heaven."

"It's too bad he can't marry all the women," Penelope mused.

Christopher and his brother sent her twin stares of disbelief.

"What did you just say?" Nick asked.

"Trial and error," Penelope explained. "A perfectly reasonable method of scientific deduction. Spend an appropriate amount of time with each until you find the one that fits."

"Exactly how long is the appropriate amount

of time to stay married?" Nick growled as he pulled his future bride into his arms for a kiss.

"Forever," she giggled. "But we found the right match. Your brother is still looking."

Christopher considered her proposition. "I think providing an appropriate amount of time with each potential candidate is exactly what the matchmaker is trying to do. Letting me see what works."

Penelope's sharp gaze focused on his. "How are things going with Gloria?"

Where to begin?

She was maddening. Beautiful. Frustrating. Thoughtful. Overly cautious. Overly whimsical. Completely incomprehensible.

At his silence, Nick's jaw dropped. "You haven't fallen for the matchmaker, have you?"

"She has the wrong name for every single constellation," Christopher said. "And she refuses to follow a simple recipe when she cooks."

"That's a firm 'no,'" Nick whispered to Penelope. "Chris is married to rules."

"I enjoy having order in my life," Christopher protested. "Don't act like you're different, just because you used other rules. You liked the clear-cut expectations that came with being a rake. I enjoy the comfort of understanding the systems around me."

"Systems are good," Penelope agreed. "Plants wouldn't be green without chlorophyll. Everything would die without oxygen."

"Courtship isn't life or death," Nick reminded her.

She shrugged. "It can feel like life or death. I was very upset when I thought you were still raking other ladies. You lads are more alike than you think."

Christopher and his brother exchanged dubious glances. "Alike how?"

"Restlessness," she answered immediately. "Nick's restlessness meant constantly changing women. Yours means constantly changing location. But eventually you'll find the one that you want."

"He'll find the right woman or the right location?" Nick asked.

"Both," Penelope answered. "Maybe. It's not an exact science."

"Maybe you're right," Christopher said. "Perhaps this village isn't where I'll find what I'm looking for."

"You're definitely looking in the wrong place." Nick turned to Penelope. "He spends the entire night staring up at the stars. There are better uses of one's time."

"Not lately," Christopher reminded him. "My telescope is still broken. Is there a jeweler in town who might—"

"Gloria can fix that," Penelope said. "She can fix anything."

"She did fix my pocket watch," he admitted. "But a telescope is infinitely more delicate. This particular one is the newest model available, both rare and expensive. I cannot risk—"

"Gloria can do anything," Penelope repeated.

"She even helped design an alarm that can be heard through soundproof walls."

Nick groaned. "Gloria did that?"

"Listen to this." Penelope jumped up from the dining table and dashed toward the kitchen.

Nick slanted Christopher a long-suffering look. "I blame this on you."

"Blame what on—"

A deafening racket rent the air, like a thousand hammers banging a thousand pots inches from his eardrums.

Penelope appeared in the doorway and pointed over their heads with a self-satisfied expression. *"Gloria."*

At least, Christopher presumed she said *Gloria.* He couldn't hear himself think over the mind-splitting cacophony.

"Fine," he shouted. "I'm going. But this racket isn't convincing me she should be anywhere near my telescope."

His brother and Penelope stared back at him without comprehending a word.

Christopher beat a hasty exit before his head could explode.

The next thing he knew, he was at Miss Godwin's front door. But he left his telescope tucked safely in his carriage.

Madge beckoned him in without a word.

He wasn't certain whether he was meant to see himself to the parlor or follow her down the corridor. He did not wish to be left behind, so he chose to follow the maid.

Miss Godwin was just inside the kitchen,

touching her fingertips to a heavy round cloth hanging from a sturdy hook. Presumably, the fragrant ball was the concoction one hoped would result in an edible pudding.

God help them all.

"Since you're here," she said, "I deduce you did not fall in love with Virginia."

"I am not in love with Virginia," he agreed. "My apologies. Am I impossible to work with?"

"Everyone is fussy when it comes to love." She lifted a shoulder. "Sometimes love doesn't care and sticks you with whoever Cupid fancies. Other times, we can help things in the right direction."

"I like right directions." He inched closer to the drying pudding and touched his fingertips to the cloth as Miss Godwin had done.

Her eyes took on a strange sheen and she glanced away.

"If I'm to drive you into the arms of your beloved, I need a little more guidance. If we discount 'passion for travel' and 'love of facts' for the moment, where should we focus our attentions?"

An extremely fair question whose answer Christopher was becoming less certain of by the day.

"I could content myself with someone… sensible," he said at last.

Miss Godwin scrutinized him. "You prize rationality above all else?"

That wasn't wrong, but it also wasn't exactly right. He thought back to his parents' unhappy marriage. "I just… want someone who can be counted on."

Her warm brown eyes filled with a surprising amount of empathy. As if she understood all too well how deeply misplaced trust could wound.

Who had hurt her? A strange anger simmered inside Christopher's chest, as if he would find the villain and do him violence.

She broke their gaze.

"To clarify," she said, then cleared her throat. "You've never met Miss Olive Harper?"

He shook his head. He was good with names. Miss Harper's was not one he recognized.

"Perfect." She glanced over her shoulder. "Grab your scarf, Madge. There's a chill in the air today."

Christopher followed them to the door.

At first, it had seemed almost silly that a matchmaker should ensure a chaperone's constant attendance. Lately, he had become particularly glad for the maid's presence. It kept him focused on finding the right match.

Not on Miss Godwin.

As they all piled into the carriage, he turned to face her. "Where to?"

"The same road as the le Duc residence." She pointed up ahead. "The Harper land is on the outskirts of town."

He nodded his understanding. Only one road led up the mountain to this cozy village. He must have glimpsed the Harper estate on his way in.

As soon as they passed the smithy, however, Miss Godwin commanded, "Turn left."

Christopher complied out of surprise. "Left? This is a trail, not a street. You said Miss Harper lives on the southbound road out of town."

"She does," Miss Godwin agreed. "Don't worry. We're not breaking any rules. We're taking a detour."

He stared at her. "A detour inherently means deviating from the expected path. Doing so without provocation is—"

"Christmas trees," she exclaimed in delight, leaning into him to point at the evergreen forest straight ahead. "Most families haven't adopted Queen Charlotte's Germanic customs, but those who wish to decorate a tree on Christmas Eve come here to collect them."

He closed his eyes and breathed in the crisp, pine-scented air. "I can only imagine what it must be like to bring an evergreen inside one's home."

"You don't have to imagine," she said with a laugh. "Go caroling on the twenty-fourth of December, and you'll see them all firsthand."

He opened his eyes and turned toward her.

Her upturned face was still a mere breath from his.

"I don't even know where I'll be in December," he said softly.

"I know where I'll be," she answered. "Right here. Taking part in tradition. Enjoying Christmas. Don't you have traditions?"

"The only one I have is never to stay more than a month in any one place," he admitted.

He had always believed the freedom to bounce about at will afforded him a privileged life.

She was making him wonder if he was missing something by trying to have everything.

"Besides, I'm not fit for caroling. Your neighbors do not want to hear me sing," he said, and the spell was broken.

He sent a surreptitious glare over his shoulder at the maid who was supposed to be watching them.

Madge batted her eyes at him innocently.

Gloria motioned for the chariot to continue down the snow-packed trail. "This path brings us up to the rear of the Harper estate. See those horses up ahead?"

He did see those horses up ahead.

The pieces clicked together. He had not met Miss Harper, but he had certainly heard of her horses. "Is this the stud farm?"

Miss Godwin nodded. "It is indeed. Although it legally belongs to the Harper family, Olive has acted as matriarch to the studs her entire life."

"'Matriarch' is the wrong word," Madge whispered. "She's the madam of a horse bordello."

Miss Godwin ignored this.

"You want someone who can be counted on?" she asked. "Look no further than Olive Harper. Practical? Yes. Well-versed in stallion facts? Yes. More than due for a holiday? Yes."

"She sounds perfect," Christopher admitted. Yet he leapt from the carriage with less enthusiasm than expected.

They made their way past the primary residence to a fenced-off section, where a talented horsewoman in a smart riding habit gentled an enormous, all-but-rabid stallion. Christopher would not have approached without three layers of armor.

"Gloria!" Miss Harper said in pleasure. "Don't come any closer. Blitzen has learned to jump the fence."

All three of them halted in place.

Miss Harper pulled a carrot from her pocket and led the kicking, whinnying stallion back to the stable. Moments later, she exited the other side, brushing off her hands as if that lovable scamp Blitzen had delicately lifted the carrot straight from her palm.

Miss Godwin stepped forward. "Allow me to present my good friend Miss Harper. Olive, this is Christopher Pringle."

"How do you do?" Christopher said automatically, but his ears still rang with Miss Godwin's words.

My good friend.

For some reason, it had not occurred to him that her role as matchmaker required her to introduce eligible gentlemen to other women. Women that were her friends. Women that were not superior to her, just different.

He wondered how often her clients' eyes

turned from prospective brides to the match-maker herself.

"I recognize the chariot, naturally." Miss Harper stepped around them. "What lovely grays! You cannot have rented them in a posting-house."

"I didn't," he agreed with a smile. "These poor beasts live in London all year, and I thought they deserved a holiday."

"Of course they do," she said with a nod. "I'll buy them from you for five hundred pounds apiece."

"What?" He took a step back.

"She's bamming you." Miss Godwin rolled her eyes toward Miss Harper. "Olive, tell him you're teasing."

"I'm teasing if you want me to be teasing." Miss Harper flashed a dimple and slid a glance over his shoulder. "May I?"

He gestured toward the grays. "Be my guest."

In no time, his horses were nibbling bits of carrot from Miss Harper's hands.

"Does she carry a pocketful of vegetables everywhere she goes?" he whispered to Miss Godwin.

"Sometimes she carries orangutans," Miss Godwin whispered back.

A startled laugh choked from his throat.

"I don't know why I asked you," he said. "You invent your answers."

"Doesn't it make a better story?" she replied unrepentantly. "Imagine her pulling a monkey from her reticule and handing it to your horses."

He shook his head. "Orangutans aren't monkeys."

"There you go again," she sighed. "Ruining perfectly good imagination with unnecessary facts."

He grinned at her.

When Miss Harper finished exclaiming over his handsome horses, Miss Godwin stepped back a discreet distance to allow them a semblance of privacy.

Over the next quarter hour, Miss Harper engaged him in delightful banter about the downsides of having a brother, the joy of finding one's passion, her dream to one day ride camels in Morocco just to see if she could.

He could practically feel Miss Godwin thinking *I told you so* as their conversation ticked every requirement he had demanded.

But he was finding it difficult to concentrate on Miss Harper, no matter how perfect she seemed in theory. Or perhaps because she fit too neatly. There were no questions, no mystery, no surprises. She was exactly what he was looking for.

He just didn't seem to want it.

Miss Harper glanced over her shoulder to gauge the sun. "It's getting late. Would you like to come inside for tea? I'm as peckish as my horses."

Miss Godwin nodded and opened her mouth.

"No, thank you," he said before she could interrupt with a *yes*. "I don't wish to outstay our welcome. It was lovely to meet you."

"It was lovely to meet your horses," Miss Harper replied with a cheeky grin, before turning and striding back toward her home.

"Well," Miss Godwin demanded. "Does Olive meet your standards?"

"Yes," he admitted as he helped Miss Godwin up into the carriage. "I had to hold myself back from proposing on the spot."

The sparkle faded from her eyes. "As I thought. You'll make a wonderful couple."

They remained silent during the ride back to her cottage. When they arrived, she scrambled from the carriage and hurried toward the front door.

Christopher hesitated. He should just drop her off as planned. Definitely not come inside.

She reached the first step.

"I have a broken telescope," he blurted out.

She paused with her fingers on the door handle. "With you?"

He nodded. "With me."

"Bring it here," she said, and disappeared inside.

Kicking himself, he dug the cloth-wrapped package from its hiding spot behind the rear squab and hurried to follow her.

The door had been left ajar. He nudged it open and stepped inside. Neither Miss Godwin nor her maid were anywhere to be seen.

He closed the door and hung his hat and coat

on the rack before venturing toward the corridor.

"I'm here," he called out. "With my broken telescope."

"I'm here," she called back from a room just beyond the kitchen.

He approached with caution, and then all but dashed inside like a child arriving at a fairy kingdom.

"You have an observatory?" he said in wonder.

"A miniature observatory," she demurred. "A makeshift private chamber I use for observatory-like activities."

It was not a grand room, but it was perfect for its purpose. A telescope stood on a wide platform in the center of the room. The large window directly above it opened at an angle, allowing an unobstructed view of the night sky whilst protecting the viewer and his device from the elements.

"This is splendid," he heard himself babbling. "I never expected you to have…"

When he finally tore his gaze from the skyward window, the true nature of her telescope jumbled his thoughts. It was not a "serviceable unit." It was not a "respectable device." It was the exact same precision-forged, incredibly expensive model as the one wrapped in linen under his arm.

His jaw fell open. "How on earth do you have a—"

"You expected me to use one of those?" She

motioned across the room toward a retired telescope that had been the height of efficiency twenty years prior.

"Something like that," he admitted.

"You weren't wrong. It's just not my only machine." She lifted a shoulder. "My father purchased that one for me when I was a child. I bought a replacement more recently." She gave him a crooked smile. "I wanted my best chance at seeing the heavens."

"You have good taste," he said, matching her lopsided smile with one of his own.

He handed her his wrapped parcel.

She grinned when she unveiled its contents.

"Ten minutes," she said. "I'll have you on your way with your telescope in working order."

"You're fortunate to have a permanent place to keep yours." He admired the dais. "I've investigated the best spots on the castle roof, but they aren't protected from wind or inclement weather. Brilliant idea to build this room."

"It wasn't me. It was my father." Her voice softened. "This was his observatory, and then it was *our* observatory."

She didn't add, *and I will share this observatory with my children*, but she didn't have to. The faraway look in her eyes spoke for her.

Christopher swallowed. This was more proof that he should take his telescope and walk away. She didn't just have ties to this village, she was anchored to this very room.

He smiled wryly. Perhaps that was why she

had taken him to see the evergreens. To show him her roots ran just as deep.

"Oh, obviously," she muttered as she settled behind a small workstation to inspect his telescope. She glanced up, said, "Easy as pie," and immediately returned her focus to the task before her.

He gazed at her, spellbound.

She pulled a pair of odd spectacles out of a drawer. One side bore a single glass, the other a series of interconnected lenses not unlike a telescope. Or a microscope.

Christopher braced himself against the inevitable surge of trepidation when she exposed the expensive device's delicate innards, but none came.

He trusted her, he realized. She might say fantastical things, but if she gave her word, she did everything in her power to keep it.

Her talented hands made short work of a complicated mess. In less than the predicted ten minutes, everything was back together, her tools put away, and her spectacles returned to their drawer.

There was no reason at all to feel a pang of disappointment. He should be thrilled. This was his cue to leave.

"All done?" he asked.

"Almost." She moved her perfectly-centered telescope to one side of its platform and placed his on the other half. "Get the window?"

He climbed atop a small ladder that had

clearly been left for that purpose, and pushed the skyward window open.

The sun had set enough not to be straight overhead, but nightfall was still hours away. Nonetheless, a sliver of a crescent moon was already visible in the sky. He grinned at her. With their telescopes, they would be able to see so much more.

He leapt down from the ladder and took his place beside her. Their hips and shoulders touched as they lowered their eyes to the lenses. His telescope was in excellent working order. She was a genius.

His jumbled brain, on the other hand... No matter how hard he concentrated his gaze through a series of perfectly functional lenses, his vision barely registered.

He did not feel the hard metal cylinder beneath his fingers, but the warm curves brushing tantalizingly against his side. He could not concentrate on picking out stars from the heavens, because his mind had filled with the scent of her hair. Or perhaps it was the scent of her skin. He suddenly wanted to know everything about her. To press his mouth to her cheek, to her hair, to her lips.

"I have to go," he said hoarsely.

But he didn't move away. He turned toward her.

She glanced up from her telescope and froze when she discovered her face scant inches from his. Froze, but did not move away, either.

There was that scent again. Lavender, or perhaps lilac. Something soft and floral and feminine. Something that could envelop him, just as he wished to envelop her in his arms. Bury his fingers in her hair. Crush his mouth to hers.

If only she wasn't the exact opposite of what he needed.

He jerked his head backwards before he made a mistake that they would both regret.

"I should go," he said again. His voice sounded tinny, as if it no longer belonged to him. "Thank you for fixing my telescope. And for sharing your viewing platform with me."

She licked her lips. "You can leave yours here if you like. To keep it safe from the elements while you're in town."

He nodded. As much because it was a generous offer as because he did not trust himself to carry expensive equipment anywhere.

Come to think of it, right now he did not trust his hands at all.

He shoved them into his pockets to keep them a safe distance from his newly repaired device—and the softness of Miss Godwin's hair—and walked away before they embarked down the wrong path.

CHAPTER 7

The following day, Christopher did not visit Miss Godwin's cottage. It was the first break in their routine since commissioning her as his matchmaker.

It could not continue. The dynamic between them was too charged.

They were each other's worst possible match, and they knew it. Yet he could not focus on other women while she was about. He shoved a hand through his hair and stared out the guest chamber window at the late-afternoon sun.

He needed a new matchmaker. Or no matchmaker at all. He ought to drive his chariot right back to the Harper stud farm and offer Miss Harper his matched grays as a wedding present. He groaned.

Life was full of ought-to-dos.

If he wanted a distraction from Miss Godwin, all he had to do was wander down into the castle's common area and walk off with the first woman who approached him. It was what his brother would've done. What his father would have done. What a thousand other men would do.

But Christopher didn't want temporary oblivion. He wanted to wed his perfect match.

If only it was as easy as ordering a telescope.

As the sunset blossomed, he could stand the wait no longer. Miss Harper it was. He marched out of the castle, summoned his carriage from the mews, and headed over to—

Blast.

He had come straight to Miss Godwin's.

She answered the door. "Did your pocket watch break again?"

He gazed at her, irritated by his own weakness. The smart play would be to cut off all contact at once. Take his telescope back, climb into his carriage, and drive away.

He did nothing of the sort.

"Is the pudding ready?" he asked as he stepped through the door.

The corners of her mouth quirked. "Have you ever made pudding?"

"Don't throw stones," he chided. "It didn't look like you knew what you were doing, either."

She watched him pass. "Where are you going?"

"To check your work."

He touched his fingertips to the fragrant cloth as he'd seen her do, and stroked his chin with his free hand as if in thought.

"No," he announced. "It needs at least another day."

She lifted her brows. "It needs another month. Once it's dry, it will last for ages."

"That's what I said." He patted the cloth. "At least another month."

She burst out laughing. "Shall I save you a portion?"

There. That took the wind out of his sails.

He would be gone in a month. It did not matter how the pudding turned out. Christopher would not be around to enjoy it.

She frowned. "Is something wrong?"

Yes. Many things.

He was in search of a suitable bride. Yet the woman he was most drawn to didn't match him at all.

He had to put a stop to this.

"About the matchmaking," he began.

Before he could continue, a loud knock sounded at the door.

Madge sailed past the corridor to answer. Moments later, the sound of boisterous caroling filled the air.

"It's February," he whispered to Miss Godwin.

"We're in Christmas," she whispered back. She looped her arm through his and dragged him toward the corridor. "Come on. Let's listen."

As soon as the carolers caught sight of her, half soldiered on with their out-of-season songs and the other half erupted in cheers.

Christopher had expected off-key drunken

warbling, but the group was far more skillful than anticipated. Several sections were sung in two- or three-part harmony. Carolers this talented did not need to practice at all. He stood by Miss Godwin, transfixed.

When the song finished, they reached for her. "Join us, Gloria! Just for a few cottages. You'll be back in time to see the stars."

She sent a wicked sideways glance up at Christopher.

"No," he said. "Absolutely not."

She grinned at the carolers. "Only if my friend can come, too."

They cheered their approval.

"I'm not caroling," he said. "I already warned you."

She ignored his protests and hooked her arm through his. "Come along, Mr. Adventure. I want to hear you sing."

He could not keep up the battle. Not with his arm looped with hers. All ability to form logical arguments fled.

She dragged him into the crowd.

"What about your maid?" He sent a startled glance over his shoulder. "Madge!"

"It's fine," she laughed. "There are thirty of us. It's just caroling."

Was anything ever just caroling?

Very well. He prided himself on being predisposed for any adventure. Certainly, he could handle this.

"Is this your carriage?" asked one of the young ladies.

"Not any old carriage," said one of the young men. "It's a le Duc chariot, if my eyes don't deceive me."

"Excellent suggestion," he whispered to Miss Godwin. "I'll follow behind in my carriage."

"In your chariot," she corrected. "And you'll do no such thing."

"You'll drive me?" he asked hopefully.

She shook her head. "I've never driven anything. Nighttime is definitely not the moment to start."

His face fell. "Pity."

As they walked to the next cottage, Christopher found himself surrounded by young ladies.

"Mr. Pringle, what do you think of my new bonnet?"

"Mr. Pringle, will you walk with me?"

"Mr. Pringle, I waited for you the other night. Did you lose my note?"

Good God. He stared at the fluttery-eyed woman in dismay. It was she of the calling card with printed directions to her bedchamber. It would be difficult to pretend he had not understood the message.

"He's not a rake," one of her friends whispered loudly. "He's bride-hunting."

That got the attention of every other female in the group. Those not already familiar with his particulars were quickly put to rights within the space of a few whispers.

Never before had Christopher wished so fervently that people would start singing carols.

He glanced around for Miss Godwin. She

was hanging back, allowing his unwanted admirers to pick him apart like crows upon carrion.

In as gentlemanly a manner as he could, he squeezed his way past the flirtatious faces until he reached her side.

"I see you don't need me to matchmake," she said, her face inscrutable.

"I…" *don't want you to matchmake at all.* Not a good start. He tilted back his head and pointed toward the sky. "Look, it's Auriga, the charioteer."

"No, that's a dunce," she corrected with a straight face. "You can tell by his odd hat and petulant expression."

"We're knocking!" yelled a voice up front as they reached the next house.

In moments, the group erupted into song.

O come, all ye faithful…

Miss Godwin's boot jabbed into his leg. "Sing."

He sighed. She asked for it. He joined in with the final refrain.

"You *do* know the words," she said as they walked to the next house.

"I have lived through two-and-thirty Christmases," he pointed out. "I know many words. Did I acquit myself somewhat?"

"Let's see how you do at the next house." She curled her fingers about his elbow. "Look, there's The Great Walking-Stick!"

"That's Canis Minor." He glowered at her. "Good God, woman. I cannot believe you use

England's most advanced telescope in order to not learn about the stars."

She grinned up at him. "I'm idiosyncratic."

"You're insane." He jabbed his finger back up to the sky. "Please try. That one there is—"

"We're singing!" came the cry from up ahead, immediately followed by *Here We Come a-Wassailing*.

To his surprise, Christopher was enjoying himself immensely. At least until the following house, when he overheard Miss Godwin's words.

"On the twelfth day of Christmas, my true love gave to me... Twelve droll devices, eleven piping puddings—"

"That is *not* how it goes," he hissed in horror.

She held her hand to her lips and whispered, "I'm singing the revised edition."

He stared at her. "That is not the revised edition. That's utter hogwash. You're making it up on the spot."

"I don't remember the words," she admitted. "It's either invent my own or not carol. And which would be the greater tragedy?"

"Gloria," yelled one of her friends. "After caroling, let's play Snapdragons over at Susan's house!"

She gazed up at Christopher. "What do you say? Are you any good at eating raisins set on fire with brandy?"

There was nothing he wanted more than to spend time with her. That was the reason why he could not. His actions would make promises he couldn't deliver. Like becoming part of her community. Like staying a part of her life. Like anchoring himself to one spot.

He shook his head.

If she was disappointed, she did not show it. Perhaps she had guessed his answer before she extended the invitation.

He had not been as certain what he would say.

CHAPTER 8

*W*hen Mr. Pringle failed to present himself for matchmaking the following afternoon, Gloria could not help but recall her friends' less-than-subtle reactions to discovering him in the market for a wife.

Perhaps he no longer required the aid of a matchmaker. Certainly, no unwed young lady in this village intended to allow him to be lonely. Perhaps he was in his true love's embrace right this second.

She tried to scrub the image from her head by rereading one of her favorite travel journals.

It didn't help.

She rearranged the solar system in her orrery. It didn't help, either. She checked on the pudding.

It definitely didn't help.

She needed answers. With an aggravated sigh, she grabbed her pelisse and set out for the castle. He liked fact-finding missions? Well, now she was on one.

It was too early for supper and too late for tea, but the dining area positively frothed with single young ladies wearing pastel gowns and hopeful expressions. It could only mean one thing.

Mr. Pringle was within.

Gloria eased her way into the dining area and took one of the last remaining seats at a far table.

Perhaps she had misread the situation. Perhaps Mr. Pringle wanted nothing more but to escape to her house for some nice matchmaking, but the buzzing cloud of shameless hoydens surrounding him would not let him leave.

She clenched her teeth. Any chit who would throw herself so blatantly at a man simply because he was charming and handsome and funny and adventurous and single…

Gloria dropped her face into her hands. *She* was one of the shameless hoydens. Jealous because she, too, wanted a chance at love.

Specifically, with Mr. Pringle.

"I heard he never stays anywhere more than a month," whispered a voice.

She lifted her gaze. It appeared she was sharing a table with a gaggle of gossipy wallflowers.

Wonderful.

"He's already been here three weeks," said another. "We've little over a sennight left to catch his eye."

"He'll never see us through that ocean of hussies," lamented another.

Gloria could not dispute the logic. The situation was worse than she thought.

"Isn't he a fine catch? I would adore a husband who loved to travel," gushed one of the wallflowers. "I would have him take me to Rome."

"Madrid," said another.

"Paris," said a third.

"We are at war with France," Gloria burst out. "Do your idyllic holidays include a trip to the guillotine?"

They all stared at her.

She jerked her gaze away just in time to hear one of them whisper, "He would definitely take his bride to Paris if she wanted to go."

Gloria set her teeth. It was probably true. He'd speak his flawless French, charm everyone in sight, and whisk his new wife anywhere she pleased.

She crossed her arms and forced herself to face a hard truth. Her irritation wasn't that he had impossible standards.

It was that she didn't meet them.

He did not need her help to find a willing bride. If she wanted to matchmake someone, she ought to start with herself. Stop waiting around for Prince Wonderful to appear, and go find him.

In fact, she would do just that.

She pushed to her feet and surveyed the common area. The unmarried ladies were here because of Mr. Pringle. The eligible bachelors were here because all the single women had conveniently gathered in one place. Gloria started forward.

One of them had to be her perfect match. Someone smart, someone sweet, someone local, with no intention to leave Christmas—or her. Someone who didn't care how she made her pudding or what names she gave the stars. Someone completely unlike Christopher Pringle.

She felt his gaze upon her before she even turned around.

He was on the opposite side of the crowded dining area, surrounded by women, and yet he had somehow glimpsed her rise to her feet. Or sensed that she was in search of someone else.

Good. She avoided danger. Everything about him was dangerous. She wasn't promised to him as anything other than a matchmaker.

If she could arrange her own match, she could put paid to her silly mooning over the wrong man. She would simply have to find someone safe.

As best she could, she flitted from table to table with a smile and a kind word for all her single male neighbors.

She could practically feel Mr. Pringle's glare stabbing into her back.

She ignored him.

When her meandering path brought her closer to his harem, she glimpsed a male neighbor at the next table. Perfect. She sat down, careful not to position herself with a direct view of Mr. Pringle.

"We missed you when we were out caroling last night," she began with a smile.

From the corner of her eye, she glimpsed Mr. Pringle gather what appeared to be a pile of bread and cheese into a large serviette and whisk an unused tablecloth from a neighboring table.

Her mouth fell open. What on earth was he—

"Meet me on the roof," he whispered as he passed.

A wave of disappointed women trickled in his wake as he strode from the dining area without a backward glance.

She made light conversation with her neighbor for as long as she could stand, then excused herself and all but ran up the winding staircase leading to the closest roof access point.

Mr. Pringle was there waiting. He had spread the tablecloth on the landing as though it were a picnic blanket. He was seated on the opposite side of a serviette piled with bread and cheese.

"I forgot to grab wine." He held up a palm. "I hope you'll sit anyway."

She did not.

Her legs trembled too badly to trust them to take her anywhere but directly into his arms.

"We shouldn't be doing this," she stammered. "You're… a client."

"I officially renounce the contract," he said, his voice grave. "As of this moment you are not my matchmaker anymore. Agreed?"

She swallowed hard, her pulse pounding. "Then, what's this?"

"I don't know," he said honestly. "Do you want to find out?"

She sat down across from him. The serviette of cheese would have to act as chaperone.

"Would you like to eat?" he asked.

She shook her head. "I don't think so."

He tied up the bread and cheese and moved it aside. Now there was nothing between them.

She gulped.

He leaned back onto the cloth, his knees propped before him. Elbows at a casual angle, he laced his hands behind his neck and gazed up at the sky. "Look. The stars are coming out."

Slowly, she lay back and linked her own hands behind her head. It should be cold. Instead, she could feel his heat.

They would be lying within arm's reach of each other if they hadn't quite sensibly given their arms something else to do. She tried to focus on the stars.

"There's Cassiopeia," he pointed out. "Her stars are easy to remember. Alpha, Beta, Gamma, Delta, and Epsilon."

She felt herself relax. "I believe you mean Agnes, Beatrice, Georgiana, Dorothea, and Edith."

Gloria could practically feel him roll his eyes. She couldn't keep the grin from her lips.

He gestured with the tip of his boot. "That one is Orion. I suppose you think the stars of his belt are named Tom, Dick, and Harry?"

"That's not a belt," she said. "Those are the buttons of his fall. They're uneven because he ate so much Christmas pudding, his gut is bursting."

Eyes crinkling, he propped himself up on one elbow to face her. "Why are you like this?"

"Blame my father," she said with an unrepentant grin. "He taught me to let my imagination run wild."

"Did he run out of time to teach you anything else?" he inquired politely.

She swatted at his arm. "Father was who taught me not to wish upon a star, but a constellation." She pointed at the sky. "I named that one *Duke* and have been wishing on him ever since."

He shook his head. "You don't get to just name things."

"Somebody gets to," she said. "Why not me?"

His gaze stayed focused on her. "What is it you wish for?"

She kept her eyes facing the heavens.

"For most of my childhood," she said at last, "I wished for Father to come home safely. It worked every time. Until it didn't."

"I'm sorry," he said softly. "That must have been hard."

She gave a bitter smile. "He was a navigator, and then a Navy Captain. He told me the stars were for finding one's way home. When he didn't make it back, I feared it was because he was seeing the wrong things. That the names and stories he'd been taught were wrong. When it mattered most, none of them helped him home."

To her relief, he did not try to give her platitudes about *these things happen* and *it must've been his time to go*. According to the society pages, he had lost his own father a few years back. He knew what it was like.

Instead of words, he slid his hand across the tablecloth and linked his pinky finger with hers.

Her heart clenched. It was the most perfect thing he could have said.

They lay there gazing upwards in silence until a streak of white slashed across the sky.

They both sat up at once.

"Did you see that?" she gasped. "It looked like a comet. Do you know its name?"

A laugh startled from his throat. "I have no idea."

She clasped her hands together in excitement. "Then I get to name it because I saw it first." She cupped her hands about her mouth and tilted her chin toward the sky. "I dub thee… 'Duke.'"

His mouth fell open. "You cannot give two astral bodies the same name."

She pointed at Draco in triumph. "So, you agree that one is already named Duke?"

"*Aargh.*" He buried his face in his hands.

"In that case it's still my comet, and I name her… Vixen."

He jerked his head up. "You can't name a comet 'Vixen!'"

"Where are you getting your rules?" she asked innocently.

"Science?" he countered.

She waved a hand. "Bah. When has science helped anyone?"

"You are completely barmy," he said. "Has anyone ever mentioned that you are stark, raving mad?"

"Besides you?" she asked. "Only everyone who's ever come on the sky-walk."

"I don't doubt it," he said. "Your complete lack of celestial knowledge would fit right in over in London. Did you have a Season?"

"One," she said softly.

He frowned. "I cannot imagine you unsuccessful at attracting a suitor. Any man who took the time to get to know you—"

"I did have a suitor. But after he sailed off to make his fortune, neither the contract nor my charms were enough to bring him back."

His lip curled in contempt. "What could possibly be more important than *you?*"

The unintentional sweetness of the question squeezed her chest with surprising power.

Pride did not allow her to list the innumerable attractions her suitor had found more attractive: India, adventure, money. Anything but a marriage to her.

"Perhaps he still plans to return someday," she attempted to jest.

His dark gaze was hot on hers. "He doesn't deserve the chance. Please tell me you are not waiting around for that imbecile to saunter back into your life."

She shook her head. "Not for a long time."

"Good," he said fiercely, and slanted his mouth over hers.

She melted into him. He was incensed on her behalf, every muscle tensed as though preparing to leap up to protect her from harm right here and now. But his kiss told another story. His mouth hadn't come to hers in anger, but desire. As though the electricity building between them had struck to galvanize them together.

He cradled her face in his hands. His kiss was not tentative or polite but raw. A blatant claiming. Not a bright spot in the night, but a sky full of shooting stars. Instead of promises, each kiss demanded complete possession. She was happy to oblige.

She parted her lips and offered him more. He wasted no time in tasting her. In proving once and for all how right the wrong man could feel. His kisses were potent. Drugging. She gripped him for strength—and because she didn't want the kisses to stop. He tasted like danger and romance and possibility. As though the stars had come out just for them.

At last, he lifted his lips from hers. "Miss Godwin…"

"Gloria," she corrected. Or meant to. It came out as a peep.

He smiled and touched his forehead to hers. "I'm Christopher, and I would very much like to keep kissing you."

She reached for him. "Please do."

The new kiss was different than the last. Gentler. Sweeter. Capable of stealing both her breath and her heart.

Yet she dare not take such a risk. No matter how enthusiastic her kisses, it would not be enough to keep him. A stolen moment was all this could be. He was a man that could not be moored.

When the tide drew away, he would go with it.

CHAPTER 9

*G*loria was cleaning the gears of the parlor clock when the knock came on her front door. There was only one person it could be.

Christopher.

Here to talk about last night's kiss.

She took a deep breath and opened the door.

"How's the pudding?" he asked as he edged around her to head toward the kitchen.

Very well. She inclined her head. No talk. Just pudding.

He reappeared, apparently having reassured himself of the pudding's continued well-being. "Grab your bonnet."

She frowned. "Why?"

He lifted her pelisse from the rack and held it out. "Come and take a ride with me."

"A ride where?" she asked suspiciously.

"Bonnet," he prompted.

She slipped into her pelisse and snatched her bonnet from its chair. "Madge!"

He shook his head. "No room. I've rented a phaeton."

She stared at him in horror. "One of the le Duc's high-perch racing phaetons?"

He tightened the ribbon of her bonnet beneath her chin. "Ready for adventure?"

"You expect me to voluntarily climb into one of the le Duc's racing phaetons?" she repeated in disbelief. "They are considered some of the most skillful drivers around and I've lost track of how many times they've crashed during races."

"We won't race," Christopher promised. "We'll just drive."

Madge poked her head around the corner. "Wouldn't do her any harm to have an adventure outside one of her books."

"Go away." Gloria shooed her out of the parlor. "You're not helping."

Christopher lifted her chin. "You said you won't leave Christmas because you don't like risk."

"France is a war zone," she pointed out. "Reasonable people don't go on holiday in war zones."

He grinned. "I'm not planning to drive you to Paris. I'm not certain my horses can swim that far."

"Under no circumstances will I go anywhere near a body of water," she said firmly.

"Noted." He gave a sharp nod. "I'd also like to point out that a phaeton is not a seafaring vessel. It is meant for short jaunts about town on nice days. This is a nice day and a nice town." He held out his elbow. "Come jaunt with me."

"Take a small risk," Madge hissed from the corridor. "The le Duc lads rarely break any bones."

Gloria took a shaky breath and considered her options. If she said yes, what was the worst that could happen?

Broken bones, as Madge had so helpfully pointed out. Mangled limbs. Death.

What did she risk by not going?

Adventure, as Madge had also pointed out. A beautiful afternoon with the very gentleman she'd spent all month dreaming about. Life itself passing her by.

"Everything carries risk," Christopher said gently. "Nothing always works out. Life is about doing it anyway."

"Not your most confidence-inspiring speech." She elbowed past him onto her front step.

There was the phaeton. The whip-fast death machine.

A tiny, open-air passenger basket fully exposed to the elements teetered high atop two rickety springs barely wide enough to connect their reckless driver to four uneven wheels—two smaller ones up front near the horses, and two enormous ones at the rear.

Only a madwoman would climb inside.

"Beautiful, isn't she?" he said with a self-satisfied smile. "May I help you up?"

Gloria glared up at the phaeton. Without

help, it would be impossible to get in. They should take that as a sign to stay home instead.

She gave a tight nod.

He grinned and managed to sneak a peck to her cheek as he swung her up and into the phaeton.

Her face heated. She had not been prepared for *that* risk.

He leapt up beside her and expertly led his horses down the snow-dusted road at an impressively sedate pace.

"What do you think?" he asked.

"I didn't know phaetons could go this slow," she answered with a tentative smile.

He lifted the reins. "Shall I spur the grays faster?"

"No!" She grabbed his arm to stop him before she realized he was teasing.

"Look around," he said. "Five minutes and perhaps six feet later, and we're still alive. The phaeton is still standing. All our bones are intact."

"For now," she muttered.

"See?" he said. "New things aren't inherently bad. This is how I feel when I travel. The unknown can be exhilarating."

"I agreed we were still alive," she reminded him. "I never said I found this contraption exhilarating."

"Let me see if I can change that," he said and tossed her the reins.

"Eek!" she squeaked, throwing her hands

into the air as if the reins would burn like acid. "I said I've never driven before!"

He gave her a placid smile.

The horses plodded forward.

She scooped the reins from her lap and tossed them into his.

He crossed his arms, tilted his gaze to the sky, and began to whistle as if he hadn't a care in the world.

The horses kept clomping.

She snatched the reins from his lap with shaking hands. "As soon as we stop, I'll kill you."

"Then you would be more dangerous than the phaeton," he pointed out. "Don't be hypocritical."

"The phaeton is my spirit animal," she said. "And my least favorite constellation. Now tell me how to drive it."

He grinned. "First, relax. Horses can sense the driver's state."

"Then we're dead," she moaned. "Didn't anyone ever tell you not to hand the reins to someone who can't drive?"

"Many people," he said with a straight face. "This is my first time bending a rule. It's a risk for both of us. Please don't crash or I'll never do it again."

"Beast." She lifted her chin.

He curved his hands over hers and adjusted her grip. "Hold the reins this way. If you want the horses to turn left, move like this…"

The slow-moving horses listed in an easterly direction.

"And if you want them to turn right, move the reins like this…"

The horses began to plod and in a westerly direction.

"And if you want them to race hell-for-leather—"

"No!" she squeaked.

"Good." He sat back. "These aren't racing horses. They would do their best and then sputter out in a trice."

He taught her how to pull the reins to practice stopping and starting, then helped her guide the horses half a mile down the road before turning around by the evergreens.

He paused the horses, then rubbed his thumb against her cheek.

"How are you feeling?" he asked softly. "Was it too much? I wanted to give you a small adventure, but I didn't mean to frighten you."

She stared back at him wordlessly.

Every nightfall, she tilted her face to the sky and wished upon her Duke. Gloria was done waiting for the stars. Life was too short. Last time, Christopher had kissed her. This time, she was going to kiss him.

She placed her hands on either side of his face and pressed her lips to his. This was dangerous. This was reckless. She was perched high in a phaeton, her mouth locked on a gentleman who would be gone within a week. Her hands trembled. She held on tighter.

His mouth was firm and familiar, his kisses hot and deep. As though he, too, had dreamed of nothing but tasting her once again. Of their bodies cleaving so tightly together that nothing could tear them apart.

This was not playing it safe. This was teetering at high speed. Leaping head-first into deep water. Perhaps the only thing that waited on the other side was more heartbreak.

She wasn't certain she was brave enough to find out.

CHAPTER 10

*M*adge opened the front door for Christopher as he was still striding up the walk.

He grinned at her, then turned to hang his hat upon its usual spot on the rack.

"I presume you've come to check on the pudding," Madge said as she closed the door behind him. "You know where to find the kitchen."

Christopher was halfway there before he realized the maid was right. Checking on the pudding's progress had become a daily ritual. As though this cottage was starting to feel like home.

Frowning, he dipped his nose to the fragrant cloth and went in search of Gloria.

She had not been in the kitchen or the front parlor. Nor was she in the observatory. He hesitated before tapping on any strange doors. He didn't wish to burst in on her in her unmentionables.

To be sure, he might *wish* to spend some

quality time in her bedchamber, but he would never presume to—

She popped her head out of a new doorway. "There you are! Come on in."

He perked up. Perhaps wishes could be granted after all.

When he stepped into the room, however, he was greeted not by a boudoir but something even better.

"You have an *orrery?*"

Awestruck, he rushed forward and ran his hands across the excellent craftsmanship of its waist-high mahogany housing with engraved-brass detailing.

The orrery's ornate, glass-topped lid rested on a side table. The open surface exposed a perfect model of all eight planets in the solar system, from Mercury to Ceres.

"Does it work?" he asked in wonder.

She gave him an arch look and engaged the switch.

Before his eyes, the planets began rotating in perfect trajectories, the ring of each orbit ever wider than the last. At the sight, his body flooded with childlike joy.

He turned to her in awe. "Where did you get this?"

"It belonged to my father." Gloria disabled the switch and pulled a handful of tools from her apron pocket. "Stay there. Watch what else it can do."

He watched in horror as she immediately

dismantled the exquisite machine. Gooseflesh rippled down his spine.

He reached out to stop her. "What the devil are you doing?"

"Taking it apart," she said, as if that was something sane people did. "I'll fix it, don't worry."

"It already worked," he protested, his voice faint.

"Bah," she said. "That's just one way to orbit."

Despite the still-stinging trauma of witnessing the complete demolition of the most exquisite machine he'd seen in his life, Christopher could not help but admire his fetching agent of destruction.

Black tendrils bounced about Gloria's face as she leaned into the orrery's innards. She nibbled her plump lower lip in concentration as she rearranged bearings and replaced gears. Her round backside tilted tantalizingly in his direction.

He had never seen anything so erotic. He shoved his hands behind his back to keep from reaching toward her.

"How did you become so clever with devices?" he managed, his voice hoarse.

"Practice," she answered. Her derrière gave a pert little wiggle. "When the stars aren't out, a lady must come up with *something* to do."

He cocked his head. "I assumed you spent your days matchmaking."

She shook a finger above her head. "You're my first."

"I'm your what?" he choked out in surprise. "You're not actually a matchmaker?"

She slammed a stubborn piece in place with enough force to rattle teeth. "I told you. I agreed to do this as a favor for Penelope."

"I know, but…" He stared at the back of her head. "I thought…"

With a final torque of some recalcitrant piece, she replaced the protective panel and swung upright.

"First client," she said as she wiped a speck of dust from her nose and smiled. "How am I doing?"

He lost the battle and kissed her.

Her mouth was sweet and welcoming. As though his inability to keep his passion in check was not a surprise, but a delight. As if even while she worked on her machine, her body had been attuned to his, just waiting for his touch.

He was happy to comply. In fact, all he could ever think about was kissing her again. Now that her mouth was once again his to plunder, his brain had shut down completely.

His senses were immersed in the joy of kissing her. The sweet scent of her hair, the soft warmth of her curves, the welcoming heat of her mouth. She was the engineer of his self-control's utter downfall. He hoped it would never end.

"I'll take that as complimentary," she said when they came up for air. "Stand back. This may shock and amaze you."

Christopher wasn't certain he could handle much more shock and amazement.

She flipped the switch.

The miniature planets that had so recently looped about each other mirroring the same trajectories as their namesake celestial bodies… had now lost their minds.

The sun rotated around Jupiter. Saturn had become a satellite of the Earth. Mercury shared its orbit with Mars.

"What did you do?" he choked, aghast.

"Do you like it?" She patted the edge of the orrery. Venus gave a drunken wobble in response. "I like to imagine this is what it looks like when the planets have a holiday."

He sagged against the wall. "Have you ever met a fact you couldn't turn upside-down?"

"Not once," she said cheerfully. "Did you check on the pudding?"

"The pudding is fine," he said. "I should be checking on the state of the entire known universe."

"Rules are meant to be broken," she assured him.

"That is the opposite of what rules are meant to do." He held out his arms toward the miniature planets. "You turned your beautiful orrery into an abomination."

She gave him a peck on the cheek and whispered, "It's a model. Models need holidays, too."

He hooked his fingers through hers and tugged her into the parlor. "Step right up. Let me introduce you to the nice books on your bookshelves. Right here we have…"

Delight flooded him to spy the explorer he idolized among the names on the spines. Not only had Christopher purchased every travel journal the man had published, he'd read each one again and again until the pages came apart in his hands.

In fact, that man was the reason Christopher's upcoming trip had become the culmination of decades of dreams. After years of correspondence, the venerable explorer had offered to accompany Christopher on a once-in-a-lifetime personal tour. Every detail was in place. Soon, he would have the sort of adventure he had previously only experienced in books.

But he had not dragged Gloria to the parlor to brag about an upcoming trip. The most important resource he intended to force her to acknowledge were the books dedicated to astronomy. She did not need to memorize entire shelves, but it wouldn't hurt for her to know actual information about the stars. She might even consider adding occasional facts to her sky-walk lectures.

Christopher selected a familiar tome on astronomy and settled on the sofa to begin. This one had clear text and plenty of illustrations. It would be an excellent introduction to the real constellations.

He patted the seat beside him. "Sit with me."

"Boring," she said when she saw the title in his hand. She spun to kneel before the bookshelf. Moments later, three slim volumes filled her arms. Only then did she join him on the sofa. "Let's start with these."

He rifled through her choices. "These aren't books on astronomy. These are travel journals about the Kingdom of Italy."

She nodded and tucked her head against his chest. Her hair smelled of sweet lilac. "Tell me something that's not in them."

He wasn't certain where to begin. "What sorts of things do you already know?"

"Fifty years ago, the Trevi Fountain was built in Rome. Eight years ago, Napoleon declared himself King of Italy." She paused to think. "Antonio Vivaldi wrote hundreds of concertos, many for the violin. The architecture has been termed 'baroque.' There's a great deal of... food?"

"None of that explains how it feels to be there." He set the books on the floor and wrapped his arms about her to cradle her to him.

She fit so perfectly against him, as if their bodies had been created for each other. He never wanted to leave this sofa.

He tried his best to concentrate on Italy. "All the people and places are so different. Do you want to start with food?"

She nodded.

"In Tuscany," he began, "nothing warms one's stomach on a cool night like a steaming bowl of *ribollita*, filled with chopped vegetables and bits of bread. In Arezzo, you can eat plump balls of *gnudi* made with cheese and spinach and drizzled in a rich sauce."

"Mmm," she murmured. "It sounds delicious."

He did his best to recall all the different local cuisines he had sampled and describe them to her in as much detail as possible. The rich creaminess of *gelato*, the spicy tang of *arrabiata* tomato sauce on pasta, the sweetness on his tongue after a sip of *limoncello*.

She nestled closer. "More. Tell me about the wine."

No chianti on earth was as potent as her touch. The soft curves pressing against him were more drugging than any wine he'd ever known. Each happy sigh made his heart beat too fast and his mind empty of everything but her. He was hers to command.

"One cannot say anything about wine without starting with grapes," he said when he found his voice. "The vineyards in Umbria…"

He held her close as he described everything he could remember about the harvesting of grapes and the countless varieties of wine. More than a man could taste in a single holiday. Or a man *and* a woman. He wished he could transport Gloria there at once in order to sample the dizzying array of flavors in person.

"And the art?" she asked when he finished.

"The *art*," he said in rapture. How she would love the art. He longed to show her. "The first time my breath was stolen from me, was by a

Renaissance fresco soaring high above my head…"

By the time he finished answering all her questions about his travels, his voice was scratchy and the hour had grown late. He hadn't noticed the passing of time.

With every memory he shared, the old vague yearnings for someone to accompany him on his adventures had taken a new shape. He did not long for some mystery woman by his side. He wanted to share experiences like these with Gloria firsthand.

"Wouldn't you like to see for yourself?" he asked softly. "To pluck a grape right from the vine and feel its sweetness explode in your mouth? Visit the Sistine Chapel in Rome and the Gothic Duomo in Milan. Listen to the songs and stories handed down through generation after generation."

At first, he thought she wasn't going to respond.

"I like to read," she said at last. "I don't need to leave my house to visit the world."

"One literally must leave one's house in order to visit the world," he said firmly. "No travel journal exists that can fully translate an experience. A taste, a texture, a scent… You can't know unless you visit."

"Then I guess I won't know," she said, her voice hollow. "I will not step foot on a boat. I have books. I'm not missing out on much."

"Not much," he agreed. "Just adventure. And life itself."

She broke from his arms and crossed over to the window to sweep open the curtain. "Let's not quarrel. It's a beautiful night. The stars are alive."

He narrowed his eyes. *She* was the one who didn't allow herself to be fully alive. How could he make her see? "The stars are just stars. Inanimate balls of gas. You are the one who—"

She spun to face him, her cheeks flushed pink.

"They are alive," she said fiercely, eyes glittering. "You're wrong."

Hardly. Any reputable astronomy tome extolled the recent discoveries of men like Wollaston and Fraunhofer. Their work with prism spectrometers proved without a doubt the surface was comprised of gases. Stars weren't living planets. They were massive spheres of heat. Nothing could live there.

He shook his head. "Stars are dead. It isn't the point. I don't see why you can't—"

Her voice rose. "Just because you don't have the same dreams, doesn't give you the right to take away mine."

He lumbered to his feet, uncertain if he should to reach for her. "Are we still talking about stars?"

Her chin trembled.

"Your constellations come from science. Mine come from my heart. That doesn't make them wrong." She jabbed her finger to the window-glass. "What's the name of that one?"

He suspected he was about to give the wrong answer. "Gemini?"

"*No.*" She blinked rapidly. "Those are my parents watching over me from the heavens. Smiling down on me every night."

She lifted her chin and braced herself, as if expecting him to correct her.

Christopher would do no such thing. As a child, he would have done anything to believe his mother was still out there watching over him. Even for a single day.

He stepped closer.

She turned away.

"My father told me I could always find my way home by looking to the skies." Her voice cracked as she touched her fingers to the glass. "And so I filled the sky with things I wanted to find."

Christopher looked out the window at the two souls holding hands high above the clouds. He imagined they *were* looking out for her. No matter what name they had.

"I didn't mean to upset you," he said quietly. "I was just using science."

"When you tell me I can't have my constellations…" She swiped the back of her hand beneath her eyes. "It feels like you're taking away the last connection to my family."

He pulled her into his arms and held her close as she sobbed against his chest.

"Never," he whispered into her hair. "There's nothing anyone can do or say to make your family stop looking after you."

He would have held her all night long, but she wiped her eyes and showed him to the door. Either she was too embarrassed to let him see her cry, or he didn't count as family.

He wished he could change her mind.

CHAPTER 11

*T*he next morning, Gloria headed straight to the castle to apologize to Christopher for taking her emotions out on him the night before. He was not the reason her parents weren't coming back. He was the one person she still had by her side.

She hoped she didn't have to fight her way through a gaggle of fawning ladies to tell him so.

When she arrived inside the castle, she spied him just exiting the public dining area. She hurried to intercept him before he disappeared up the spiral stairs to the guest wings.

His eyes lit up when he saw her. "How did you sleep?"

A flush heated her cheeks. "Let me apologize for last night. My outburst—"

He brushed his fingers against hers. "Never apologize for loving your family."

She gave him a crooked smile. "This might be the first time I take your advice."

"Shall we try for two?" He proffered his arm. "Let's take a promenade."

She widened her eyes in faux shock. "You? Journey by foot?"

"Minx." He led her out of the castle and into the sunlight. "Where's Madge?"

At home. Gloria never brought her to the castle. Besides, it wouldn't matter. "When it comes to you, she's a truly terrible chaperone."

"A hobbyhorse would do a better job," he agreed.

She shuddered. "I hate the empty stares from their little wooden eyes."

He blinked. "You're scared of hobbyhorses?"

"Not scared," she said primly. "It's rude to stare with fake eyes. How would you like it if your guest chamber was filled with the vacant gazes of a thousand disembodied doll heads on wooden sticks?"

He grimaced. "Promise me we'll never try it."

She cocked an eyebrow at the insinuation that a shared bedchamber was in their future.

The sound of shouts and laughter filtered out from the woods on the edge of the castle grounds.

Gloria came to a sudden stop. Her flesh had gone cold. "Where are we going? Why are we here?"

He sent her a quizzical look. "You recognize this area?"

Too well. She gripped his arm. "The pond is in the middle of those woods. I'm not going."

"We're definitely not going in the *water*," he

agreed, his smile bemused. "It's frozen over. People are ice-skating."

"I don't ice-skate," she said. Her heart was beating too fast to let her think. "I *won't* ice skate."

He rubbed the pad of his thumb against her cheek. "You don't have to. Let's just walk by."

She swallowed. He didn't understand. The idea of being near so much water... "I haven't passed by the pond in six years."

"It's a pond." He lifted her hands in his and gave them a comforting squeeze. "You're stronger than you think. Let me prove it to you."

Strong. She was strong. No need to overthink things. She gave a jerking nod. "We'll walk by. At a safe distance."

He placed her fingers back on his arm and led her down the path.

With each step through the trees, the sounds grew louder. The shriek of a child. Snow crunching beneath her boots. The shrill panic in her head with every step closer to the frozen pond.

When they broke from the trees, the icy surface was abuzz with activity. Couples skating in complicated figures, children pushing each other in a bright red skating chair, the skate-vendor shouting out prices to passers-by.

"Do you want to get closer?" he asked.

Her legs barely held her upright

"I don't know if I can," she whispered.

He covered her hands with his. "We can try it and find out."

She flapped weak fingers toward the path. "Don't you think it's safer from the sides?"

"Sometimes," he said. "But the greatest achievements require some level of risk. Trying one's best, even if things don't work out. It can make it an adventure."

"Adventure is your peccadillo." She shook her head. "Not mine."

"Isn't it?" he asked softly. "I'd wager you've read every travel journal on your shelves. I imagine you can quote from them at will."

"That means I like to read," she stammered. "Not that I'm Christopher Columbus."

His forehead lined with disappointment. "Why did you ask me all those questions about Italy if you weren't interested in going?"

"I'm interested," she forced herself to admit. "I just can't go."

"Start smaller," he suggested. "You don't have to sail around the world in a canoe. Try something simple. Here, in your own hometown. Something you already know you can do."

"Used to do." Until the sea and its ripple effects had stolen everyone she loved.

"I'll tell you a secret," he said. "A wise person once told me, 'A good experiment focuses on all information available, not just the results you like best.'"

She slanted him a wry glance. "Was it Penelope?"

"It was Penelope," he admitted. "She's a wise chemist."

"Don't listen to her," Gloria said. "She sells perfume made of animal excretions."

He was clearly trying not to laugh. "But does it work?"

"Irrelevant," she said. "Only a crazy person wears animal fluids."

"You take risks all the time," he reminded her.

Wrong. She shook her head. "I never take risks."

"Are you sure? I've seen you take apart a complicated machine and poke about inside without a second thought."

She lifted her shoulder. "Devices are easy."

"Were they easy the first time?" he insisted.

No. She'd been alone. No one to help her. She'd had to try and try again until tears of frustration came to her eyes. Each success had felt like climbing a mountain.

"I've seen you take plenty of risks in the kitchen," he continued. "You are not at all concerned with the edibleness of the final product."

She lifted a finger in warning. "My puddings always come out fine."

"But you can't guarantee that," he pointed out. "You throw things together and hope for the best. Think of the pond like a pudding."

Gloria slid a doubtful glance toward the skaters racing across its frozen surface. The pond was nothing like a pudding. But perhaps it was a risk she should try to take. Just this once. With him.

"You took a phaeton ride," he coaxed.

"A high-perch racing phaeton," she said with a small smile. "I drove the horses."

"And lived to tell the tale," he said encouragingly.

She tightened her lips. He was right. It had been exhilarating.

"I'm not sending you out on the ice," he said softly. "I'm offering to go with you."

Her heart gave a little flip.

He wasn't choosing the water over her. He was offering to take the risk together. Like driving a phaeton. Or sharing a kiss.

She tightened her grip on his arm and hoped she wasn't making a terrible mistake. "I'll try."

His eyes widened. "You will?"

"Don't make me regret it," she warned with a weak smile.

"You won't regret it," he promised, his gaze serious. "I'll never let you go."

He procured a pair of skates for each of them and helped affix hers over her boots. Carefully, he led her out onto the ice. Her heart hammered so fast she could hear it in her ears.

Children hurtled past, heedless of her and each other.

"Don't look at them," he said. "Look at me."

He took the edges of both her hands in his and pushed his skate backward, pulling her forward just a few inches.

Darkness clouded her vision as her gut roiled in protest. "I'm going to be sick."

He stopped in alarm. "Do you want to sit down?"

She gripped his hands tighter and fought for calm. "No."

He gave another encouraging smile. "You can do this."

"I don't think *I* can do this." She sucked in a deep breath. "But maybe *we* can do this."

"I wish I could kiss you," he said in a husky voice. "You're especially kissable when you're puffed up like a determined adventurer."

She rolled her eyes. "I'll puff you up like a—"

He motioned toward their feet.

They were doing it. They had *done* it. They were out on the ice!

"I told you," he said arrogantly. "You're braver than you think."

She was so glad she was out here with him. That he'd helped her conquer a demon. "How did you know?"

"How brave and competent you are? You've been completely independent for the past six years." He skated them around a fallen twig. "You didn't just learn to fend for yourself. You taught yourself mechanical engineering. You give tours to total strangers. And you even agreed to matchmake a gentleman you didn't like as a favor for a friend."

"I didn't appreciate your presumptuous mouth." She sent a haughty stare down the bridge of her nose. "The rest of you was somewhat attractive."

He leered at her. "How do you like my mouth now?"

She tried to hide a smile. "Only when it's kissing mine."

He glanced over his shoulder and whispered, "Tell me when they're not looking."

Gloria smacked his arm. "Not here, you daft—"

Her breath caught. She had let go of his hands and was skating on her own. Keeping up out of her own volition. She was doing it!

"I'm skating," she said in wonder. A fit of giggles threatened to overtake her. She grinned up at him. "I'm skating!"

Victory coursed through her. She grabbed for his hands not because she needed them, but because she wanted to throw herself into his arms and kiss him. *He* had made this happen.

Pride shone in his eyes. "Are you sure I can't kiss you?"

"Don't tempt me," she said with a laugh. "The way I'm feeling right now, I might do it."

He grinned back. "See? You do like adventure! Is there any chance of talking you into getting on a boat with me next month?"

All her joy evaporated as sharp knives of reality crashed back over her. "Next month?"

"Next week, I mean." He rolled his eyes at his error. "I don't know how time goes so fast. One minute you're in a high-sprung racing phaeton and the next you're on a slow boat to India."

India.

The ice seemed to tilt. She stumbled blindly.

He caught her. "You're all right. I won't let you fall."

No. He already had. Gloria's throat went dry. She had been wrong. The danger didn't come from the ice at all.

It came from the gentleman who held her hands in his.

"—a bucket of good fortune," he was saying. "I've been dreaming of this trip for years. When the man whose travel journals I so greatly admired agreed to act as my personal guide, it was a dream come true. A once-in-a-lifetime opportunity that's finally going to happen."

Gloria's stomach heaved. She knew exactly what was going to happen. Once he left, he would never be back.

The sea would swallow him whole.

"You bought passage?" she made herself ask. "Y-you have a ticket already?"

He patted his jacket pocket. "Won't let it out of my sight. I'm not looking forward to a six-month voyage, but I can't wait to step foot on land. The subcontinent has so much to explore. Who knows how long it might take! I'll secure return passage once I know what port I'll leave from."

Or never come back at all.

India tended to have that effect.

Her chest grew tight. In the best-case scenario, the ferry ride alone meant he would be gone for over a year. Her throat stung. Whether he realized it or not, he was never coming back to Christmas. He'd said it himself: there was too much world to explore.

"Can we leave?" she whispered. "I'm done with the ice."

He gazed at her with obvious affection. "Anything you want."

She could not even offer a brittle smile in return.

He could give her nothing she wanted. She had only herself to blame. From the moment of his arrival, she'd always known he planned to leave.

Now she knew it was going to destroy her.

CHAPTER 12

"*I*t's Miss Quincy's turn!"

The group of vivacious carolers were seated in a large circle in the middle of the local jeweler's drawing room. Christopher grinned at Gloria from the other side of the boisterous circle.

As soon as Miss Quincy had been properly blindfolded and moved to the center, the entire company rose and scrambled to new chairs. This time, Christopher ensured he took a seat next to Gloria.

"Your friends share your disreputable tendency to completely ignore rules," he whispered. "I distinctly spied Miss Borland peeking beneath her blindfold."

Gloria's smile was wicked. "All's fair in war and Blind Man's Bluff."

He narrowed his eyes. "That is not how that saying goes."

"Shhh." The others shushed them.

After exchanging one last grin, Christopher

and Gloria straightened their spines and made themselves perfectly still.

One of her friends dashed forward to tap the Blind Man and run away. The others grinned at each other in anticipation of great fun.

At first, Christopher had not known what to make of Gloria's invitation to tonight's gathering. She had seemed far more shaken than he had hoped by the trip to the ice-skating pond. When they arrived here tonight, she had seemed distant. Disappointed.

He had pushed her too far. Guilt gnawed at him. He had wanted to prove to her that she could expand her horizons, not accidentally encourage her to close her walls tighter.

But over the past hour of parlor games and spiced wine and rowdy friends, she seemed to forcibly push away whatever was bothering her. The smile slowly returned to her face, and the teasing tone to her voice. He was glad to have her back.

She pointed at the current Blind Man and whispered, "Go tag him!"

As Christopher darted across the room, tapping the newest Blind Man's arm as he passed, the rest of the company scurried to exchange seats with each other.

After waving his arms about for a moment, the Blind Man stumbled in Christopher's direction and managed to knock his shoulder with the back of his hand with a suspicious lack of false starts.

Christopher shook his head. Cheaters, every one of them.

"Pringle's turn!" roared the crowd.

He rose to his feet and crossed to the center of the circle. As the previous Blind Man began to cover Christopher's eyes with the blindfold, he forced his cheeks into the widest smile possible. He kept the manic expression in place as long as he could.

Only when the brush of a hand passed behind his elbow did he drop the exaggerated smile and allow his cheeks to sag. The corner of the handkerchief dipped just enough to allow him to spy Gloria racing to take a seat amongst the others.

"I see you peeking!" The warm peal of Gloria's delighted laugh warmed his heart. "Did everyone see that? He broke a *rule!*"

Christopher held out his arms in front of him as if the blindfold weren't sliding down his face and pantomimed a wooden stumble in her direction.

She was laughing too hard to hide from his outstretched hands.

"Fair to say he got her," someone shouted in glee.

"I think that's enough Blind Man's Bluff for one night," their host said with a chuckle.

"Back to the wine," someone else called out.

A resounding cheer sounded at once.

Christopher ripped the blindfold from his head and tossed it upon one of the newly vacated chairs.

Gloria was staring up at him with an inscrutable expression.

"May I fetch you a glass of wine?" he asked.

She shook her head and rose to her feet. "The stars are out. Walk me home?"

"With pleasure." He would take her anywhere she wished to go.

They took their leave from the high-spirited company and made their way out into the silent night.

"Did you enjoy the party?" Gloria asked as she curved her fingers about his arm.

"Very much," he admitted.

Christopher had met many of the tourists that came and went from the castle, but after spending a few occasions with Gloria's friends he began to notice that not all of the locals stayed local. Some of her friends had seasonal homes elsewhere. For others, their seasonal home was the one here in Christmas.

He loved the idea of having a close circle of friends, yet having the freedom to flow in or out of that circle as one wished.

Gloria pointed up at the sky. "That one looks like a Venetian gondola."

"It looks like Lacaille's Reticulum to me," he said with a chuckle. "You'd be able to tell the difference if you visited the Continent."

"I'll never leave Christmas," she said without breaking stride. "Besides, I've always been able to tell the difference between the stars." She began to point. "There's Auriga and Columba and Lepus..."

"Wait." He came to a complete stop. "You *do* know the constellations?"

Her eyes twinkled up at him. "Of course. Don't you?"

"But you... I..." He could not even form words.

She tugged him to keep walking.

"I learned the stars long before I learned devices," she said. "I'm our town's resident expert. You met me during the second lap of the sky-walk, where we use our imaginations. On the first lap, which you missed, my group learns traditional constellation names and scientific star designations."

Heat climbed the back of his neck and he groaned out loud. "I am the worst blackguard."

"You did make insulting assumptions about my intelligence, competence, and general fitness for speaking to children." She tossed him a pointed glance. "And delivered your public judgment in the most mortifying way possible."

Good God, he had been a fool.

"I am appalled by my 'gentleman astronomer' prejudices." He winced. "I don't know how you can forgive me."

"I already accepted your apology," she reminded him. "Back when I agreed to be your matchmaker."

"I didn't realize what I was apologizing for back then," he said. "Now I do. I'm sorry."

As they approached her doorstep, she paused and gave him a half smile. "Madge pointed out that I may have been a wee bit severe on you, too."

He felt himself brighten. "Madge likes me?"

Gloria opened the front door and gestured inside. "You don't see her anywhere, do you? She's hoping you'll compromise me."

"So am I," he said fervently. "So am I."

She tossed him a saucy look over her shoulder. "I'm still considering it."

"What?" He chased after her. "You've been having carnal thoughts about me?"

"I'll let you know when I decide." She pressed her finger to his lips and turned away.

His head swam. Or maybe that was his blood, rushing to his trousers at once.

Christopher was thrilled not to be the only one hoping for pleasurable adventures in their future.

So thrilled that he belatedly realized he was still wearing his hat and coat. He jogged back to the front door to place his outerwear on their customary spot on the rack, then returned to the kitchen to visit the plum pudding.

It wasn't there.

He swung his gaze up to the ceiling in confusion. The hook was there; the pudding was not. He turned in a slow circle, darting searching glances about the kitchen. One hook. Zero puddings. A mystery.

"Where's the pudding?" he called out.

Gloria appeared in the corridor but did not immediately answer.

A strange frustration gnawed at him.

"I come in, I hang my coat, I bid 'good day' to the pudding." He motioned up toward the empty hook. "No pudding. Did you eat it?"

She crossed her arms in silence.

"Did you give it away?"

She lifted her brows.

"Did you hide it from me?" he asked in exasperation.

Gloria tilted her head. "Maybe."

"What on earth for?" he demanded.

She stepped closer.

"This feeling you're experiencing, this lack of equilibrium... The sensation that something is missing, that something is wrong, that something is not as it should be... That a part of your life is incomplete and no longer fits? That's how I feel when you take away something comforting to me. Something familiar." She paused before adding, "Amplified by a thousand."

"It's a pudding," he told her. "I was surprised, perhaps, but it didn't leave a hole in my heart."

"It made a small one," she said. "Just for a second. Think back. You had a ritual. Something familiar that made you happy. And I took it away. Why do you think you cared?"

It was more than a ritual, he realized. Her cottage had begun to feel like a home they shared together. The empty spot left by the pudding made him realize how big of a hole *she* would leave if he lost her, too. He had not liked the sensation at all.

Before he could answer, she ducked out of

the corridor for a moment and then reappeared with the pudding.

"It was in the observatory," she said as she hung it back on the hook. "I didn't mean to hide it from you. I felt like the observatory was more 'ours' than the kitchen. So, I thought you might like to keep our pudding close."

He wanted to keep *her* close for as long as he could. He longed to share much more with her than pudding.

Heart pounding, he pulled her into his arms and kissed her. This time, he was not thinking with his shaft or even his brain, but something deeper. More powerful. Every time his tongue touched hers, an answering flicker of something stronger, something sharper, something infinitely more terrifying, unfurled in his chest.

He wanted more than kisses. More, even, than a night of torrid passion. He wanted to know that every time he reached for her, she would be there. If the disappearance of a pudding made him dread the loss of a single shared moment with her, what the devil was he going to do without her on a six-month trip to India?

It was the opportunity he'd dreamed of. He would never turn it down. But it would no longer be a dream come true if he couldn't bring her with him. She was beginning to feel as much a part of him as his own soul. The question was whether she felt the same.

He lifted his mouth from hers. His pulse galloped out of control.

"I would love to show you the world." He

hesitated, unsure how to put his thoughts into words, or what exactly he intended to propose. Perhaps they could figure it out together. "How would you feel about joining me on an adventure?

Her gaze did not rise to meet his. "Maybe someday."

Not the enthusiastic response he'd been hoping for. He tried to take heart. *Someday* was not the same as *No*. There was still time to change her mind.

"You should see her trunk," came a dry voice.

He leapt away from Gloria. "Madge! I didn't see you."

"I hide even better than pudding." She pointed down the hall as she walked away. "Bedchamber is that way."

"What the devil is she talking about?" Christopher swung his startled gaze toward Gloria.

Her cheeks were bright red. "I'll show you."

He followed her to an open door at the end of the corridor. Inside the airy chamber was a tall wardrobe, a demure bed, and a large wooden trunk.

Gloria retrieved a key from the wardrobe. It quickly unlocked the trunk. She gave him a long, searching look and then flipped open the lid. He braced himself.

The trunk appeared to contain a variety of gowns, an array of shoes, a selection of bonnets, and at least two lacy parasols.

"What am I looking at?" he asked.

She let out a long sigh. "Venice. Madge and I packed for Venice. Our itinerary changes every few weeks and we repack. We're thinking of going to Sicily next."

The trunk took on new meaning.

"You pick a place," he said slowly. "You read everything you can about it, gather the ideal supplies in order to have the perfect trip, carefully pack each item in your trunk... and then you don't go."

She blinked a glassy sheen from her eyes and nodded. "It's our ritual."

It wasn't a ritual. It was a cage.

His chest tightened.

This was the true Gloria. Ice-skating and phaeton rides were as far outside her comfort area as she would ever go. He liked her more with every passing hour and it didn't matter. This was as close as she would let herself come to adventure.

"Here," he said. "I'll help you pack for Sicily."

She began pulling items from the trunk and placing them in careful piles atop her bed.

Day dress, evening dress, cape, spencer. Hair brush, tooth powder, tiny soaps.

"Where in Sicily will you and Madge be traveling?" he asked.

Her eyes went wide. "Everywhere?"

"Then you're missing a few items." He opened both doors to her wardrobe and peered inside. "You need a bathing outfit for the beaches. And the warmest fur you own if you plan to scale Etna."

"Does it snow there like here?" she asked as she added a thick scarf to the trunk.

"Not year-round. But, yes, there can be ice on the mountaintop and hot sun at the beach on the same day."

"It sounds amazing," she whispered.

He handed her a pair of dancing slippers to add to the trunk. "It *is* amazing. You'll love it."

Except she wouldn't. This trunk would never leave her bedchamber.

His heart sank.

He couldn't stay, and she wouldn't leave. They weren't a perfect match at all. They couldn't even make a devil's bargain. She wouldn't try to force him to give up his love of travel, and he would never tear her from the comfort of her home.

Their chance for a future together was as make-believe as the "holiday" they were packing for.

No matter how much he wished it were real.

CHAPTER 13

Gloria locked her freshly-packed trunk and hung up the key.

Making-believe with Christopher had simultaneously been a great diversion and bittersweet torture. She wished she could pack with him for every trip. That someday... one could even be real.

But the mere thought sent butterflies of panic beating inside her chest.

She yanked the blanket from atop her bed. Gloria could no longer stand to be in the same room as her unused trunk. "Come with me."

He followed close behind as she led him into the observatory. "What are we doing?"

"Having a picnic." She handed him the blanket and relocated the telescopes to a safe corner of the room.

Her heart sped. Their futures might be destined in opposite directions, but their paths had not yet diverged. For as long as he remained, she intended to follow their attraction wherever it might lead. She couldn't keep him forever, but she would hold him close every moment they still had.

Starting with tonight.

When she bent to lift the wooden platform in the center, Christopher tossed the blanket aside and rushed to take the dais from her. "Where does this go?"

She motioned. "Lean it against the far wall."

As he did so, she dragged a carpet to the center of the room below the skyward window and centered the soft blanket on top.

She gave him a lopsided smile. "I didn't think far enough ahead to pack bread and cheese in a handkerchief…"

"Serviette," he murmured with a little cough. "I found it very romantic."

So had Gloria. She rummaged in a hidden corner. "But I do have this."

She pulled out a large bottle of brandy and placed it in the middle of the blanket.

"All liquor, no food," he said with a straight face. "I like how you picnic."

She plopped down onto the blanket and motioned for him to join her. "This is the pudding's brandy. There's barely more than a swallow left for each of us, but I hope we can make do."

"We'll find a way," he assured her, and settled beside her on the blanket.

She uncorked the bottle and inhaled the brandy's sharp, sweet scent. "Shall we toast?"

"To anything you wish." The corners of his

mouth curved in amusement. "This is your picnic."

"In that case…" She lifted the bottle up high as though it were an offering to the heavens. "To the stars!"

She took a healthy swig and then handed him the bottle.

"May they ever shine upon us." He lifted the bottle high.

She nodded her approval.

He followed her lead with a shot of brandy, then swirled the empty bottle with a chuckle.

"You were right," he said with a chuckle. "Just enough for two sips."

"Just enough," Gloria agreed. She took the bottle from him and set it aside, well out of harm's way.

She placed her hands on either side of his chest and pushed him flat onto the blanket, then cuddled up beside him so that both their faces tilted up toward the stars shining high above them.

"You already know how I became interested in the heavens," she said after a long moment of companionable silence. "Why did you?"

"Same reason," he said. "Or the opposite. My parents."

"Your father was a Royal Navy Captain?" she teased.

"My father was a flash-tempered Narcissus," he said, his voice devoid of humor. "I learned to stare out the window at the stars as hard as I could, in order to pretend I couldn't hear the shouting."

Aghast, she slid her hand beneath his and interlaced their fingers. "He sounds dreadful."

"He excelled at dreadful," Christopher agreed. "When Mother left us, her absence destroyed me. But I couldn't blame her for going. All I wanted was to escape, too."

"And you've been escaping ever since," Gloria said softly.

He swung his head toward hers with startled eyes. "I'm not escaping."

She arched a brow. "Aren't you?"

He shook his head. "I stopped running away a long time ago. I'm searching for something better. At first, I needed a place where I could go unnoticed. Later, I wanted to find a place I could belong."

"And now?"

"Now I like exploring," he said with a lift of his shoulder. "You may not have heard this, but it turns out, adventure is fun." His voice turned wistful. "Seeing all the different ways to live one's life helped me feel better about mine. I started making small changes. Picking up new ideas wherever I went."

"Like French?" she asked

"More than French." He seemed to think it over. "It's not just language or food or customs. It's an alternate way of viewing the world. Of treating each other. Of enjoying each day. I learned to be grateful for things I might never have considered before." He paused. "Traveling doesn't just make me a better person. It makes me… *happy*."

She gave his hand a squeeze. "You deserve joy."

He gave her hand an answering squeeze. "Everyone deserves joy."

"I'm happy!" She turned her head toward him and let him see the truth in her eyes. "I'm happy every time I'm with you."

She stuck out her face and pushed her lips into an exaggerated pucker as though trying to kiss him without bothering to actually move closer.

He gave a snort of laughter and bent his neck down far enough to kiss the tip of her nose. "You are the strangest woman I have ever met, but I like it."

She sighed with pleasure. "You say the sweetest things."

His voice was droll. "Finally, a woman who appreciates my finer talents."

"Speaking of talents…" She pointed up through the window at the stars. "What do you see up there?"

"Is this a test?" he asked suspiciously.

She nodded. "It's definitely a test."

He squinted up toward the heavens. "Hydra?"

"Wrong." She affected grave disappointment. "That's clearly a lady's hair ribbon."

"Is that so?" He pointed at a different corner. "What do you see over there, Resident Lady Astronomer?"

"A harpsichord." She moved his hand in the

direction of Ursa Major. "And that set of stars over there look like… three French horns."

He wrinkled his nose in obvious disagreement. "Hens."

She jerked her eyes toward his. "What?"

He pointed up. "Not horns. I think they look more like chickens."

"You see three French hens up there in the sky," she repeated in disbelief. "*You*."

He widened his eyes at her. "Doesn't everyone?"

"What I see right now—" She let go of his hand and rolled atop him. "—is a man I like very much."

He curved his hands about her hips. "What are you going to do about it?"

She answered by slanting her mouth over his.

Her heart pounded with pleasure. A thousand roses would not have been a greater gift than his three French hens.

Christopher was bending a rule, just for her. He wasn't merely allowing her to be herself, no matter how silly that might be, but actively joining his imagination with hers.

She'd like to join a few more bits together.

He was temptation incarnate. Everything about him was something she shouldn't have or couldn't have, but wanted very much. She sank her fingers into his hair as she kissed him.

His lips were firm and generous, his tongue hot and demanding. She would relinquish anything he wanted if he would give her everything she needed. Her body yearned for him, from her banging heart to the rush of desire racing through her blood. She might lose him on the morrow, but she would not allow tonight to pass them by.

"Tell me about your travels," she murmured between kisses. "Do all cultures require cravats?"

He murmured *No* without separating his mouth from hers.

She slid her fingers from his hair down to his neckcloth. In moments, she untied the knot. With a flourish, she tossed the soft square of white silk aside.

"Tourists," she murmured. "Always with the neckcloths. Tell me about this very interesting coat of black superfine." She ran her hands over his hard muscles. "Do men in all places hide their gorgeous arms in such things?"

"They do not," he said between kisses. "Horrid custom."

She wriggled her skirts up so that she could better straddle his thighs, then pulled him upright in order to divest him of his coat. When she'd dreamed of what it might be like to undress him, she hadn't realized her fingers would fumble with each button because her hands trembled so. Or that removing each layer of clothing would feel like stripping away another shield from her heart.

When the well-tailored superfine and accompanying waistcoat joined the forgotten neckcloth outside the blanket, he moved to lay back down.

She stopped him.

"This linen shirt," she said as she ran a fingertip along his shoulder. "It offends my sensibilities."

"A thousand apologies, madam." He removed the shirt in a single fluid movement.

Her breath caught. Having him to command was headier than any brandy. Seeing his naked flesh with her eyes, feeling his strong thighs trapped beneath hers, made her feel more powerful than any star in the sky. He wasn't looking at his telescope. He was looking at her. Submitting to her every wish because his desire matched her own.

His hot gaze never wavered from hers. "How else may I be of service?"

She touched her fingers to his muscled chest and ran her hands over its hard contours. Her imagination had not come close to describing how fine this man would look half undressed. And the way he felt to the touch... Her core throbbed in anticipation of having all of him at once. But first, a few layers remained in their way.

"This wretched gown I am wearing," she said with an exaggerated pout. "Some imbecile named Ackermann designed its closures so that they could only be opened by a maid."

"I don't see a maid anywhere," he said gravely. "Shall I do my best to rescue you from this horrific prison of satin ribbons and figured muslin?"

She nodded. "I would be eternally grateful."

"Turn around," he commanded.

She complied at once, her pulse thrumming with excitement. She had not realized that following orders could be even more erotic than giving them. Her hands trembled as she lifted her skirts to straddle him completely. The sensitive spot between her legs felt at once shockingly exposed and yet too far away. She wanted more.

"Come closer." His voice had gone thick.

She scooted back until her derrière pressed against the flat planes of his stomach. Her pulse skipped. She was now straddling the direct proof of his arousal. She tried to catch her breath. The knowledge that he wanted her as much as she wanted him only made her desire grow even stronger.

"Hurry," she whispered.

"No," came his arrogant reply.

Slowly, inch by inch, he slipped each scrap of ribbon through its eyelets. As he exposed each small morsel of flesh, he lowered his lips to her bare skin in a kiss.

Her skin shivered deliciously each time.

His mouth was hot and deliberate as lips traced a sensuous pattern down her spine. He was treating her as if they had all the time in the world to get to know each other's bodies. As though she were a precious package meant to be savored. As if they were not just building toward a physical union, but creating a memory of pleasure so profound that it would last an entire lifetime. Each brush of his hand, each mind-drugging kiss, etched itself deeper onto her soul.

When at last the final eyelets had been exposed, he tossed the satin ribbon aside. He pushed her puffed sleeves and the straps of her loose shift down over her shoulders. Her arms were trapped at her sides and her bosom was a hairsbreadth from being fully exposed.

"Don't stop," she begged.

In answer, he slid her sleeves down over her elbows, releasing each trembling arm one by one.

"Now what?" she whispered. "Shall I turn back around?"

He pressed his lips to the base of her neck. "Not yet."

As his mouth left a trail of kisses along the curve of her shoulders, his hands cupped her bosom and wreaked glorious torture on her sensitive breasts and nipples. She was not even facing him, and her body was utterly his to command. She expected to melt into his touch, but instead felt the delectable tension build higher and higher.

Her bent legs tightened about his thighs as her core rubbed against his thick shaft. The carnal pressure between her legs grew ever more demanding. It was a spot only he could touch. A yearning only he could fill. She could scarcely breathe from wanting him so much.

"I feel," she gasped as the uncontrollable

arousal expanded until she could think of nothing else but finding release with him. "I feel like we're still wearing too many clothes."

"I always feel that way around you," came his answering growl just below her ear. "It will be my pleasure to address our problem."

He lifted her hips from his thighs and pushed her skirts down to her knees.

She leaned back against him to kick the material away. She was almost completely naked. The chill air did nothing to cool the heat of her body or the racing of her pulse. She could not stand to be separate from him for much longer. Waiting was a sensual torture she was not sure she could bear.

"Not fair," she said as she ran her hands down his breeches. "A gentleman never allows a lady to have the only undressed body in the room."

Her rear facing him, she edged forward on her knees until she could reach his boots. She did not bother taking her time. She wanted him nude as quickly as possible.

"You're still wearing your stockings," he reminded her as he ran a finger across her garter. "Leave them on. I like it."

A spike of arousal shot through her at the realization that her body was as powerful an aphrodisiac for him as his was for her. She could hear the catch in his breath as he enjoyed the curve of her derrière… and perhaps a glimpse even lower. She had never felt so exposed or so powerful.

She tossed his stockings away with his Hessians, then turned to face him. Her breath heaved in excitement and arousal. The moment was almost here. All that remained now were his breeches.

She reached for his fall.

He caught her wrist. "Be certain. Is this what you want?"

She did not pretend to misunderstand. Her bare bosom brushed against his muscular chest. She was more than certain. Desire raged within her. For his body, and for him. This was their one chance. "Don't you want it, too?"

"I want all of you." He lifted her and placed her beside him on her back, then positioned himself between her thighs.

"I want all of you, too." She kissed along his jaw, letting him see her urgency. She wanted him to realize she'd never desired anything more in her life. He was what she'd been waiting for. She rubbed her bare hips against his breeches. "But I suspect we need to unbutton your trousers in order for you to let me have it."

"I don't mean one time," he said as he reached between them to free his shaft. "I mean all the times."

The resulting gap in his waistline caused his breeches to sink below his buttocks. She ran her hands over their muscular curves and pulled him closer. His shaft now nestled directly against her wet heat. Her breath caught.

He moved his head lower until his mouth reached her breasts.

"Are you listening?" he asked as he suckled her.

No. She was not listening. A rich, restless pressure was swirling within her.

Sensing her needs, he slid his hand between her legs and began to play.

She gasped for air. A rush of pleasure washed all conscious thought from her mind. He was not offering her the release she sought, but stoking the flames even higher. With his mouth to her breast and his hand between her legs, she was helpless to do anything more than submit completely. All she wanted was him.

His mouth rose from her nipple long enough for him to murmur, "I want you to be my partner in all things."

She slid her hands into his hair. "I want you inside me."

The corner of his mouth lifted. "I want to take that as a yes. But just in case my intent is unclear…" His hand paused its sensual magic. "I'm referring to you being my wife. Would you like me as your husband?"

Her heart skipped. She shoved her doubts away. They would deal with the future tomorrow. For now, they had tonight.

She wriggled against his hands to try and coax him to stroke her again. "Convince me."

He moved his hand away from her legs altogether.

She nearly cried out from the loss. "No, I want—"

"I'll show you what you can have." He lowered his head between her legs and introduced her to the heavens.

She closed her eyes and gave herself over to pleasure as he illustrated talents with his mouth and tongue that she had never dreamed possible. Only when her legs stopped trembling did he raise back up and realign his body with hers.

He kissed the side of her mouth. "What do you say? Do you like what I have to offer?"

"Let me show you." She wrapped her legs about him and arched her hips to nudge his shaft to her core.

He entered slowly, carefully, gently.

There was a brief moment of pain, and then only fullness and a growing yearning for more.

This was what she had been waiting for. The pleasure he built within her burned as bright as the streak of a comet, innumerable constellations filling the sky, an entire universe of heat and light and beauty. They were creating a new world together.

"Don't hold back." She met him rhythm for rhythm. "Take me with you."

He grabbed her hips and covered her mouth with his.

They did not stop until the stars exploded for both of them.

When at last they finished, he rolled over on his back and pulled her into his embrace. His heart pounded beneath her ear. Her own had escaped her chest and belonged wholly to him. She nestled closer as their breaths slowed into a gentle, lulling rhythm.

"You didn't give me a straight answer," he mumbled. "Was that a yes?"

It was definitely a yes. But before she could reply, a tiny snore whistled from his mouth.

He'd fallen asleep.

A tender smile curved her lips. She brushed the damp hair from his forehead. Was it any wonder she loved him? He was perfect, inside and out. She would give him his answer when he awoke.

Goosebumps danced along her skin. She crawled to her shift and slipped it on over her head. There was no sense pulling on her gown without being able to lace it. She rescued it from its ungainly heap and folded it as neatly as she could to keep the wrinkles at bay.

She glanced over at Christopher.

Still sleeping.

Another smile tugged at her lips. The cold didn't seem to bother him at all. However, wrinkles just might. No respected member of the *ton* would leave an assignation with the points of his cravat in disarray.

She snorted to herself as she folded the surprisingly wide square of silk. Soon, his waistcoat and linen shirt had joined the neckcloth in a neat pile. She reached for his coat and gave it a brisk shake to loosen the wrinkles.

Papers fluttered from an interior pocket.

"Blast," she muttered, and grabbed them up as quick as she could before they slid beneath a bookshelf to be lost forever.

Her triumph in this mission faded the moment she realized what she held in her hands.

His ticket to India.

No. Worse. This was a *pair* of tickets. Dual passage for himself and his bride. A year-and-a-half voyage, most of it over treacherous seas, and to him its certainty was a foregone conclusion. Her stomach twisted.

He'd called it the trip of a lifetime. An astonishing opportunity he'd dreamed of for years. It even included a personal introduction to the subcontinent by the explorer he idolized. There was no chance of Christopher cancelling such a trip.

Just like there was no chance of Gloria going with him.

A sudden tightness in her chest made it impossible to breathe. There was only one fair response to his proposal, and it wasn't the answer either of them wished it could be.

He deserved his perfect match, and they both knew it wasn't her.

Her limbs trembled at the thought of goodbye. It wasn't just that he would leave her, not just that his attraction to her could never be strong enough to make him want to stay, it was that even if he were willing to give up adventures for the sake of their marriage, she had no wish to tie him down and cause him to be resentful and unhappy.

She loved him too much to marry him.

He stirred just as she was sliding her gown back over her shift. "What are you doing?"

"We're getting dressed." She handed him his clothes in a neatly folded stack.

He was almost completely back to rights before he recalled their unfinished conversation. With an embarrassed smile, he looked up from his boots.

"Pretend I am down on one knee for reasons other than tying my Hessians." He cleared his throat and flung open his arms in grand fashion. "Miss Gloria Godwin, would you do me the great honor—"

Her heart felt as though it were being ripped from her chest. She loved him more than she'd ever believed possible. And she couldn't keep him.

"No," she whispered.

His handsome brow lined with confusion. He struggled to his feet, one boot still untied. "N-no?"

She hated hurting him. But the life she would give him as his wife would hurt him even more.

"I can't be what you want," she said brokenly, "and you can't be what I need."

"Can't we try?" he stammered.

"It would ruin everything." She swallowed hard as she faced the truth. "One perfect memory is all we can have."

CHAPTER 14

Christopher leaned against the uncomfortable bark of an evergreen trunk and gazed out at the swirling mass of laughing, happy skaters.

He had no wish to join them. He had lost his taste for skating. Or laughing. He had meant to leave Christmas on the morrow in the company of a bride.

Only one of those things would come to pass.

The matchmaking had not gone as planned. His careful requirements defining his ideal bride had been the first to go out the window.

Yet his final choice did not waver. He wanted Gloria as his wife.

His fist fell against the tree trunk. He had been smart enough to propose prior to taking her virginity, and foolish enough not to secure the answer until after it was too late.

But *was* it too late?

With renewed hope, he turned from the frozen pond. He cut through the woods in the direction of the cottages. Perhaps he had not been clear enough or romantic enough. Perhaps if he tried again, phrased things a different way, there could still be a chance.

When Madge saw it was him at the door, she ushered him into the parlor without a word.

Gloria looked up, startled. She had been reclining on her sofa with one of her travel journals.

He was tired of books. They needed to embark on the real adventure. Perhaps that was the problem.

"Is this because of India?" he demanded. That was when everything had seemed to change.

She set down her book. "Partly."

"I would never leave you." He pulled the tickets from his inner pocket and brandished them toward her. "I bought double passage. We can go together."

She wrung her hands in her lap and refused to meet his eyes.

"I can't think of anyone I'd prefer to share this opportunity with." He jabbed a finger at the spines on her shelf. "Do you see the name on these spines? We don't have to read about such wonders from books. The great explorer himself will personally show us about."

Her lip trembled. She closed her eyes as if in pain.

He hurried over to the sofa and dropped down to his knees to force her to look at him. "I don't ever want to leave you behind. I want you to come with me."

"I want you to stay here," she said in a tiny voice. "You see the problem. We are not meant to be together."

"I'll be happy to stay here," he promised her. "Multiple months out of the year if we must. But Christmas is not all there is. I can't give up the trip of a lifetime at the drop of a hat—"

"I'm a hat?" she said wryly.

He sighed. "You're an impossible bit of baggage and I want to bring you with me."

"If you knew me at all, you would know better than to ask." Her voice shook. "I've told you time and again. No boats. No water. I don't want to leave home."

"Even as my wife?"

Her eyes pleaded with him to understand.

He did not. His heart ached.

Refusing to come with him hurt as bad as being left.

He looked down at the tickets in his hands. He crumpled them into a ball and sprang to his feet.

"Fine," he said. "No India. Where *can* we go?"

She winced and looked away.

"Sicily?" he demanded.

She shook her head.

"Ireland?" he suggested

She stared at him in obvious pain.

"London?" he said desperately. "We won't have to take a boat!"

She gave another small, miserable shake of her head.

"I can't," she whispered. "It reminds me too much of… everything. That was the last time I went anywhere."

His voice rose in hurt and disbelief. "Only if I agree to never again step foot outside this god-forsaken village, only then would you agree to marry me?"

She didn't answer. She didn't have to.

His heart thudded in bitter disillusionment.

This was the "forever" she was willing to offer. No adventure. No freedom. Never leaving the radius of a single, tiny village.

It wasn't a matter of metaphorical leg shackles. If she could imprison them both in place with literal cuffs of iron, she would do it in a trice.

He looked down at the crumpled ball in his hand and unfolded the wrinkled paper back into a ticket.

This was it.

Gloria would never allow a husband to climb on a boat and leave her, and she bloody well had no inclination to board a vessel herself.

The rules were simple. Have his dreams, adventure, the life he'd always wanted… Or stay here, stuck in the same tiny corner with her.

He lifted his gaze to hers. "I can't just… wallow about playing at snapdragon and caroling for the rest of my life."

Her eyes were tortured and red. "I know."

He shoved the ticket back into his pocket and tried one last time. "Is there anything I can do to change your mind?"

CHAPTER 15

Gloria's legs shook beneath her as she pushed to her feet. This was even harder than she'd feared.

She hugged her arms about herself and wished more than anything else that their differences were nothing more complex than some device she could take apart and put back together. Find a new pattern that worked for them both.

Christopher was so sweet, so smart, so fearless. He needed to leave, and he deserved to find someone with the same adventurous spirit to journey with him. Her heart ached.

If she hadn't already loved him to the point of bursting, his presence here today would have done the trick. He wasn't trying to give her an ultimatum. He was trying to compromise. She was the one destroying her own dreams.

There was no middle ground between yes and no, between here and there, between stay and go. They were planets orbiting a closed system with precisely two states: on or off. Since they couldn't be on, that left only one choice.

She would have to be the one strong enough to make it.

"I can't go, and you can't stay." She took a scratchy breath. "That's not a marriage. That's martyrdom."

He opened his mouth.

She would not allow him to give up his soul. "Keep your ticket. Travel makes you *happy*. I will not be the cause of you forsaking your dreams." She tried to smile. "Go live them. You deserve it."

He looked at her a long moment without moving, without saying a word, without wobbling on his orbit. Without any sign of life at all. Then he turned and walked away.

There was nothing she wanted more than to chase after him. To pull him to her, bury her face in his chest and vow to stay with him for always. But where? In the middle of the vast ocean on a rocky ferry, inching toward India with no help for miles and no sign of land for months and months on end? Her flesh crawled.

All she could promise was to love him with all her heart, from right here in Christmas where she belonged.

Even if it meant living without him.

CHAPTER 16

*T*he following morning, Christopher watched in silence as the castle's footmen carried the last traces of his presence out of his guest chamber and down to his carriage.

He'd already returned the chariot, and the high-perch phaeton. It would be a long while before he had any inclination to take a jaunt in another one of those again.

He glanced at his reflection in the looking-glass. The smudges beneath his eyes would only get worse on the long trip down to London. He wouldn't sleep well for a week. Or possibly ever again.

He turned from the chamber and plodded down seven flights of stairs. His holiday was over. Huzzah. It didn't feel as though he were setting off on adventure. It felt as though he were descending the nine circles of hell from Dante's Inferno.

A purgatory of his own making.

Another footman rushed up to greet Christopher as he reached the bottom step.

"Your carriage is just outside, milord." The footman motioned toward the exit. "Your driver awaits at his perch."

Christopher nodded. All was exactly as he had requested.

He despised it.

"Thank you," he murmured to the footman, and pushed his way outside the castle.

There it was. His trusty coach. His trusty horses. His trusty driver.

A castle footman rushed forward to open the carriage door for him. "Staff has taken the liberty to place a warming brick inside so that you are not cold on your journey, milord."

Christopher stared at the cloth-wrapped brick on the coach floor. It was a thoughtful gesture.

It wouldn't make any difference.

The cold he fought did not come from the weather but deep inside his chest. Against all odds, he had finally found love. Now he was leaving, just like he'd always said he would. One month and done. Never a day longer in any one place. Mr. Adventure, off on his next journey.

Was this really the life he intended to choose?

"Sir?" the footman asked hesitantly.

"Thank you for the brick." Christopher spun away from the coach and started walking.

"Will you be back?" the startled footman called after him. "Shall I keep your brick warm?"

"I don't know," Christopher said without turning around or slowing down. "Do what you think you must."

That was what he was doing, starting right now. Doing what he must.

Gloria had accused him of running away. Of traveling not for love of adventure, but for the sake of leaving.

Even Penelope had likened Christopher's restlessness to Nick's rakish misbehavior. Flitting from affair to affair in order to guard his heart from something as permanent as love.

Perhaps Christopher had been playing the same game. Hopping from ship to ship, careful never to stay anywhere long enough to put down roots. Always in search of the next new thing because he was too afraid to risk falling in love with any one place or any one person.

He ducked his head to the wind. It didn't matter how scared he was. Love had found him. He hadn't been able to move fast enough to avoid being caught. Cupid had struck not in India or Paris or Rome or Russia, but right here in a tiny mountaintop village.

Only a fool would give up without a fight.

He banged on Gloria's front door.

She flung it open, her dark eyes red-rimmed and puffy. "Did you come for your telescope?"

He'd forgotten all about his telescope. "I came for you."

"I'm not going." She edged a half-step back.

"I'm not taking you." He took a deep breath. "I'm *choosing* you."

She stared up at him. "What does that mean?"

"It means I'm here," he said. "Right here, with you. For as long as you want me."

She bit her lip. "I thought you were leaving."

"I was looking for the place where I fit in." He held up his palms "It turns out that place is right here with you."

"I thought you wanted a wife you could travel with," she stammered.

"I'd like that," he admitted. "But I love you. You're the dream I pick."

Her expression was anguished. "You'll come to resent me. That's the last thing I want."

"I'd resent losing you," he said. "I would rather be together."

She shook her head. "What about India?"

"India will always be there." He lifted her chin with his knuckle. "I don't want to miss a single day with you."

"Neither do I," she said, her voice cracking. "But I don't want to make you give up something you love."

"You didn't hear me." He took her hands and pressed them to his heart. "I *like* to travel. I love *you*. I would give up breathing if it meant spending one more moment together."

She stared up at him, her face pale.

He lowered her hands. "If you don't feel the same, I'll respect your decision and walk away."

Even if it tore him apart.

CHAPTER 17

*G*loria pressed Christopher's hands to her galloping heart.

He loved her.

And if she couldn't find some way to meld their orbits into one, his trajectory would take him a world away. She would never have another chance.

Her mind raced. She had been wrong to think like a machine. *Yes, no. On, off. Here, there.* Between any fixed points, there was always space. One just had to look hard enough to find it.

Christopher was willing to give up everything he'd ever thought he wanted because he believed what they had was worth so much more together. She needed to be willing to do the same.

The fate of their future was the ice. Not a safe surface like the pond, frozen over with inches and inches of dense ice for stability. This was a thin wafer. A flimsy scrap of an iceberg, floating in the scariest ocean she could imagine.

She had to tie on her skates and race out to meet him anyway.

"I love you," she said in a rush, before fear could hold her back. "Sometimes I lose my breath from the force of it. I look at you and all I can think is that I never knew my heart could stretch so big to fit this much inside."

His hopeful gaze flew up to hers.

"I'm scared," she said. "Terrified, actually. But a wise man once said to me, 'If you want to move the horses you have to pick up the reins and try to drive them.'"

The corner of his mouth quirked. "Was it me?"

She nodded. "It was you."

He squinted at her. "Am I the horses or the reins?"

"You're the love of my life," she said with a choking laugh. "I don't want to live without you. Not for a single day."

His grip on her hands slackened. "But?"

"I'm not ready to get on the boat," she admitted in a tiny voice. "But if you're willing to start with something small and work together toward something big, I'm willing to start taking risks."

"Are you sure?" His eyes searched hers.

She had never been more certain of anything. "You are worth the adventure."

He straightened his shoulders. "So, in response to my earlier question…"

"Here is the answer." She pressed his hands to her lips for a kiss, then dropped to one knee. "Mr. Christopher Pringle."

His eyes sparkled. "It's actually 'the Right Honorable' but I wouldn't dare interrupt."

She smacked his leg. "*Ahem*. The following question goes out to the Right Honorable and Insufferably Pedantic Mr. Christopher Pringle, explorer of the world."

"You know, I think that *is* my full name." His warm gaze was full of love.

Her heart sang. "Would you make me the happiest of women and be my husband, now and forever?"

He pulled her up and into his arms for a kiss. "I love you, soon-to-be Mrs. Pringle."

"I love you, newest resident of our humble village." She peered up at him through her lashes. "Did you ever think you'd fall for the matchmaker?"

"I fell for you before I knew you were the matchmaker," he admitted.

"W-what?" She gaped at him in surprise.

He nodded. "When I saw you giving that sky-walk, I thought you were the most beautiful creature I had ever seen. Add that to your obvious interest in stars, your sweetness in providing such tours, the respect that everyone else clearly had for you... How could it be anything but love at first sight?"

Her mind emptied of thought. "But I... You..."

"To be clear," he continued. "That was before

I got close enough to hear the twaddle spouting from your kissable lips. Face full of cold water, that was. You ruined my favorite hobby *and* the moment, all in one go."

She burst out laughing. "Short-lived, but I'll take it. Five minutes of love at first sight is better than none at all."

He wiggled his eyebrows. "Want to try something that lasts longer than five minutes?"

She wrapped her arms about his neck. "What exactly do you have in mind?"

He carried her into the bedchamber and showed her.

CHAPTER 18

The following year

"You're back!" Nigel shouted with delight. He ran up to Gloria and threw his arms about her waist in a fierce hug. "Where did you go?"

Annie cuffed the side of his woolen cap. "London, you ninny. Down there, the Season only comes once a year."

Gloria grinned at them both. "Thank you for leading the sky-walk in my absence, Annie. I heard you were wonderful."

"I could lead the sky-walk in my sleep," Annie pinched Nigel's cheek. "This lad probably could, too."

"Then I have a treat." Gloria smiled over her shoulder at her husband. "We're going to have a different sky-walk today."

Nigel's eyes widened. "Different how?"

"One trip," she explained. "A single, leisurely stroll."

"But what about the wishes?" he stammered, his blue eyes full of panic.

"We don't have to wait for wishes anymore," she assured him. "I'll point out the true names—"

"—and I'll say the opposite," Christopher finished, joining his arm with hers. "We can have both ways at the same time."

Annie smirked in his direction. "I can't wait to hear Mr. Pringle try to use his imagination."

Gloria squeezed Christopher's arm and murmured into his ear, "One might be surprised how imaginative you can be."

Annie skipped along beside them as they headed toward the newest crop of tourists awaiting a tour of the heavens.

"Was London as wonderful as they say?" she asked.

"Wonderfuller," Gloria promised and sent a tender glance toward her husband.

She had been so nervous. First to leave home, and then to return to the place that had brought her nothing but heartache. She had been terrified of what might go wrong.

London was glorious. With Christopher, every day was full of surprises and every night full of love. The weeks became a blur of ballrooms and pleasure gardens and moonlit strolls. No wonder his friends never missed a Season. She would be thrilled to have one again every year.

To make it a tradition.

"*Sei pronta?*" he asked.

Are you ready?

She grinned. They had been working on her Italian in case she worked up the courage to one day get on a boat. "*Con te, sono pronta a tutto.*"

With you I am ready for anything.

Nigel pointed up at the sky. "Look, there's Leo!"

Annie sent a skeptical gaze toward Christopher. "What do *you* see?"

"A pair of hands scandalously interlaced." He linked his fingers with Gloria's and lifted them for Annie to see. "Like this."

She covered her eyes with one mitten. "The scandal… it scalds."

Nigel tugged at Gloria's pelisse. "Make a wish! Quick!"

She made a show of closing her eyes tight and scrunching her face hard in concentration.

When she opened her eyes, Nigel asked, "What did you wish for?"

"To visit the stars," she answered automatically.

"Mrs. Pringle might actually do it," Annie told Nigel with pride, then raced him toward the tour group.

Christopher lowered his mouth to her ear. "What did you really wish for?"

She let her mouth curve into a wicked grin. "Adventure."

EPILOGUE

Two years later

Christopher gripped the rail of the ship with one hand and held his wife close to his chest with the other. The warm sun and salty breeze buffeted them.

He lowered his mouth to nuzzle Gloria's hair. "What do you think?"

The wind whipped wild black tendrils about her face as she grinned up at him. "You were right, as always. New places are exhilarating."

She was the one who never failed to surprise him.

Once the war ended, he'd hoped she would reconsider her stance on traveling to the Continent. Only the promise of Italy had been strong enough to eventually tempt her onto her first boat.

From the moment she arrived ashore, the joy of travel had taken hold. They'd managed to tour most of the western countries between frequent trips back home.

"What did you like best this time?" he asked. "Sicily or Sardinia?"

"Actually using my trunk," she said and nestled into his chest. "The places we go don't matter as long as I'm there with you."

Christopher felt exactly the same way. He pressed a kiss to the top of her head. "Are you ready to go back home and make a new batch of pudding? I promise to try very hard not to measure things."

She shook her head. "I'm not sure we have time. I was hoping to shop for new spices."

He gave her a curious look. "Easily solved. There are plenty of spice shops in England."

She pulled out of his grasp and bit her lip as she opened her reticule. "Not *these* spice shops."

Christopher's heart leaped. He shoved the tickets back to safety before the wind could carry them off the deck.

"India?" He stared at his wife in joy and disbelief. "Together?"

She blinked up at him innocently. "Unless you want me to go by myself."

"You're stuck with me," he growled and swung her into his arms. "Forever and always."

She squealed in delight and smacked his chest. "People are watching!"

"Let them watch this," he said without a care, and covered her mouth with his.

THE END

Miss Virginia Underwood can't resist adopting strays. Her latest find turns out to be a surly, reclusive war hero recovering from his wounds in anonymity. He doesn't want her help. But he might accept something else...

Join the fun in *Never Say Duke*, the next romance in the *12 Dukes of Christmas* series!

Keep turning for a **Sneak Peek**!

THANK YOU FOR READING

Love talking books with fellow readers?

Join the *Historical Romance Book Club* for prizes, books, and live chats with your favorite romance authors:
Facebook.com/groups/HistRomBookClub

Check out the *12 Dukes of Christmas* facebook group for giveaways and exclusive content:
Facebook.com/groups/DukesOfChristmas

Join the *Rogues to Riches* facebook group for insider info and first looks at future books in the series:
Facebook.com/groups/RoguesToRiches

Check out the *Dukes of War* facebook group for giveaways and exclusive content:
Facebook.com/groups/DukesOfWar

NEVER SAY DUKE

Yes, Virginia, there is a Viscount...

Miss Virginia Underwood cannot resist rescuing a stray. Her latest find turns out to be a surly, reclusive war hero trying to recover from his wounds in peace. He doesn't want her help—and Virginia definitely doesn't want to fall in love. Not when a future with him would mean returning to the the same *haut ton* who laughed her out of Town during her very first Season.

Theodore O'Hanlon, Viscount Ormondton, sequestered himself far from London to heal in anonymity. For now, he can be himself. As soon as he returns, he's meant to wed the woman his father selected years before. But when Miss Underwood turns his carefully mapped life upside-down, Theo must decide which battles are truly worth fighting for.

The *12 Dukes of Christmas* is a laugh-out-loud

historical romance series of heartwarming Regency romps nestled in a picturesque snow-covered village. After all, nothing heats up a winter night quite like finding oneself in the arms of a duke!

Love romance? Have a free book, on me!

Sign up at http://ridley.vip for members-only exclusives, including advance notice of pre-orders, as well as contests, giveaways, freebies, and 99¢ deals!

SNEAK PEEK

Virginia glanced at the clock in the corner. "I can spare another half an hour. Tell me, what does a gentleman do when he's promised a set to a lady, but they've agreed not to dance?"

"Sneak her out to the balcony for a kiss?" Theo guessed hopefully.

She appeared to consider the idea, then shook her head. "No balcony in here."

He blinked. Would a kiss have been an option if he'd said "between the stacks" instead?

"I've never stood up with a gentleman at a ball," she said. "For dancing or otherwise. You practice whatever is done in such situations, and at the same time I will learn what it is I am meant to do."

The idea of Virginia spending her time with other gentlemen—locked in a dance or otherwise—soured Theo's stomach.

"There's nothing to practice about spending half an hour with an honorable gentleman," he said. "What you need to learn is not to be taken advantage of by a boorish suitor."

"Perfect," she said. "I'll be me, and you can be my boorish suitor."

He grabbed her wrist and tugged her into the center of the room. When she complied, he glared at her. "That was the first test. You should not have come with me."

She frowned. "This is where you dragged me."

"I'm the boorish suitor," he reminded her. "Never let the boorish suitor drag you anywhere."

"What was I supposed to do?" she asked.

He pointed at his cheek. "Slap me."

"You're on crutches," she stammered.

"Don't slap me with one of my crutches. Just slap me."

She nodded as if taking a mental note. "Anytime a loutish gentleman tries to drag me somewhere I do not wish to go, I will slap them."

"Not just dragging," Theo said quickly. "If he makes lewd comments you dislike, touches you anywhere unwelcome, acts fresh or forward in any manner at all, slap him with your glove. If you're still wearing it, even better."

She nodded. "Understood."

"Next scenario," he said. "What do you do if a scoundrel tries to kiss you?"

She wrinkled her nose. "Mostly just stand there until he finishes."

He stared at her. "Does this happen often? I

thought you'd never stood up with a man to dance before."

"Kissing isn't dancing," she pointed out. "Men needn't write their names upon one's card in order to steal a kiss."

"Writing their names upon your card is the very least that—" Theo clenched his fingers about his crutches and tried to slow his pulse. The blackguards in her past were not currently present for Theo to teach a lesson. He started again. "With the right man, you'll enjoy kissing. With the wrong one, slap him."

She made a face. "He was definitely the wrong one."

Theo tried to ignore the flash of relief at the realization that there had been only one such incident before. With Virginia, any of the usual assumptions were out the window. He wanted their first time to be perfect. Theo hadn't been this nervous about the thought of kissing a girl in twenty years. He didn't want her to look back on the memory and wrinkle her nose, but to sigh happily.

His heart skipped when he realized this meant he was thinking of their first kiss as a foregone conclusion. As inevitable as the tides, or the waxing of the moon.

"Here we go." He was glad they had the pre-text of "boorish suitor" to protect them. If he kissed her as himself, in the way he truly wanted to... Who knew what would happen?

He closed the distance between them. Their

toes were now touching. His lips could be on hers in a heartbeat.

"You're not wearing a fichu," he said. "I can look down your bodice from this angle."

She stared back up at him in silence.

"Slap me," he whispered. "That was an extremely impolite thing to say."

"You *can* see down my bodice from that angle," she said. "Do you like it?"

"I like your bosom from every angle," he growled. "That's not the point. The point is—"

Good Lord. He didn't even have to *act* to behave poorly.

Her lips curved. "I like how you look from every angle, too."

"Do not say things like that to a self-important cad," he warned her. "He'll think you mean them."

"I mean it with you." She peered up at him shyly, then glanced away. "I find you attractive."

Desire pulsed through Theo's blood. This lesson was not at all going the way he had planned.

"You are more than attractive." He could barely fight the craving to kiss her. It was more than the allure of plump red lips and long lashes over bright green eyes. It was Virginia. Everything about her was irresistible. "Scoundrels will be as captivated by you as I am. You must defend yourself."

"From what?"

"From this." He lowered his mouth to hers.

ACKNOWLEDGMENTS

As always, I could not have written this book without the invaluable support of my critique partners and copy editor. Huge thanks go out to Erica Monroe, Darcy Burke, and Nikki Groom. You are the best!

Lastly, I want to thank the *12 Dukes of Christmas* facebook group, my *Historical Romance Book Club,* and my fabulous street team. Your enthusiasm makes the romance happen.

Thank you so much!

ABOUT THE AUTHOR

Erica Ridley is a *New York Times* and *USA Today* best-selling author of historical romance novels.

In the new *Rogues to Riches* historical romance series, Cinderella stories aren't just for princesses... Sigh-worthy Regency rogues sweep strong-willed young ladies into whirlwind rags-to-riches romance with rollicking adventure.

The popular *Dukes of War* series features roguish peers and dashing war heroes who return from battle only to be thrust into the splendor and madness of Regency England.

When not reading or writing romances, Erica can be found riding camels in Africa, ziplining through rainforests in Central America, or getting hopelessly lost in the middle of Budapest.

Let's be friends! Find Erica on:
www.EricaRidley.com

46985805R00120

Printed in Poland
by Amazon Fulfillment
Poland Sp. z o.o., Wrocław